DOCTOR WHO
AND THE
WAR GAMES

Based on the BBC television serial
by Malcolm Hulke and Terrance Dicks by arrangement
with the British Broadcasting Corporation

Malcolm Hulke

A TARGET BOOK

published by
the Paperback Division of
W. H. ALLEN & Co. Ltd

A Target Book

Published in 1979
by the Paperback Division of
W. H. Allen & Co. Ltd
A Howard & Wyndham company
44 Hill Street W1X 8LB

Reprinted 1980
Reprinted 1982

Printed in Great Britain by
Cox & Wyman Ltd, Reading

ISBN 0 426 20082 9

Contents

'It is our destiny to rule. We have the superior intelligence, energy and determination to bring a New Order to all galaxies within the Universe. For this glorious crusade we shall need an army of ferocious fighting men. These soldiers we shall recruit from the most warlike planet known to us—Earth. And, having made our recruitment in large numbers, we shall ruthlessly discard all those of inferior quality. This process of elimination, in which all those who fail shall die, will be called the War Games.'

Chief War Lord

1

Sentence of Death

'What a sad, terrible place.'

Jamie, his kilt ruffled by a light breeze, surveyed a landscape of undulating mud. The utter desolation was broken only by occasional stubs of trees, dead and lifeless. He sniffed at the breeze.

'And what's that awful smell?'

Behind him stood the TARDIS, the Doctor's Time and Space machine which from the outside looked exactly like an old-fashioned blue police box. After their last adventure the Doctor had promised to try and return Jamie to his own homeland and time—Scotland in 1745, where Jamie had been fighting English red-coats in the Second Jacobite Rebellion before he had met the Doctor.

Jamie turned to the Doctor. 'This looks nothing like my country. Are we even on Earth?'

The Doctor was locking the door of the TARDIS. 'I think so, Jamie. The question is, when?'

Zoe, the Doctor's other companion and an astrophysicist from a time in the distant future, had already walked some distance from the TARDIS to explore their surroundings. She called from a rise in the ground, 'Doctor! There's something down here.' She went down the other side, out of sight.

The Doctor and Jamie followed her, squelching through the mud. They found Zoe staring at a tangle of rusted wire.

'It's not much but it's *something*,' she said. 'It's the only sign of life so far. What are the little spikes for?' At regular intervals twisted barbs stuck out from the tangled wire.

'Barbed wire,' the Doctor explained. 'Filthy stuff. Invented by an American to pen in cattle on the range, then used against human beings.'

'What's that?' Jamie pointed to an oval-shaped domed object, half submerged in the mud.

'A steel helmet,' said the Doctor. 'I think we have arrived in one of the most terrible times in the history of Earth——'

A distant rumble of heavy artillery gunfire drifted to them on the breeze. It was followed by a loud, high-pitched whine from the sky.

'Get down!' Using both hands, the Doctor pushed Zoe and Jamie into a crater, throwing himself on top of them.

Zoe shouted, 'Ugh! It's wet and filthy——'

But her words were drowned by an ear-shattering explosion less than twenty metres away. A second shell screamed down and whacked into the soft ground, sending up a spurt of flame and smoke. It was followed by a third. Then silence. The air was filled with the acrid stench of high explosives.

'You said we've landed in one of the most terrible times in history,' Jamie panted, his heart racing. 'What's happening, Doctor?'

The Doctor remained where he had fallen, lying on top of his companions. 'The First World War. It lasted from 1914 to 1918—four years when the whole of Europe went mad. Eventually, the Americans and Japanese and almost everyone joined in. They all believed they were right and that they were heroes.'

Zoe asked, 'Is it safe to get up now? I'm lying in water.'

'*I say, are you three all right?*'

They looked up. Standing on the edge of the crater was an attractive young woman in a long khaki skirt and a matching military-style jacket.

Jamie was the first to scramble to his feet. 'Where are we?'

'Between the lines,' said the young woman. 'No place for civilians. I'm heading for Ypres but I seem to have got lost. Can I give you a lift in my ambulance?'

The Doctor stood up and helped Zoe to her feet.

Over the brim of the crater he saw a khaki-coloured truck bearing a large red cross. 'That's very kind of you, ma'am, but you see——'

He stopped short. Emerging from another crater were two soldiers with spiked helmets. They levelled their rifles at the young lady ambulance driver and at the Doctor.

'*Hände hoch!*' one of them called, the German for 'Hands up.'

'Oh dear,' said the young Englishwoman. 'I'm afraid we are now all prisoners of war.' She seemed quite unruffled.

The Doctor, Zoe and Jamie sat on the floor in the back of the ambulance as it trundled along a bumpy road through wastes of mud. One of the German soldiers stood over them, rifle at the ready.

'*Wohin fahren wir?*' ('Where are we going?') asked the Doctor.

The soldier said nothing. He looked tired, hungry, and unwashed.

Jamie whispered, 'Couldn't we jump him, Doctor?'

The Doctor shook his head. 'Remember his companion is holding a gun on our lady driver——'

The ambulance stopped with a jolt. Somewhere beyond their vision shots were fired and men shouted. The German soldier jumped down from the back of the ambulance, just in time to be met by two British soldiers. Resigned, the German dropped his rifle and raised his hands.

One of the British soldiers called, 'There's three civilians in the back, sir.' He looked up at the Doctor. 'You lot, out.'

The trio descended into the road. The ambulance had been surrounded by half a dozen British soldiers. The two Germans stood with their hands clasped behind their necks, awaiting their fate. A young officer came towards the Doctor.

'I'm Lieutenant Carstairs. Are you people French or Belgian?'

'We're neither,' said the Doctor.

The officer turned to the young Englishwoman. 'Who are they? Where did you find them?'

'In No Man's Land.'

'No place for civilians. Tell you what,' Carstairs said to the Doctor, 'we'll get you to base. Lucky for you that we ambushed the ambulance. Otherwise by tonight you'd be eating German sausage. Or dead.' He laughed.

Zoe didn't appreciate the lieutenant's joke.

'There you are,' said the sergeant. 'A drop of British brew will buck you up.' He handed around three mugs of steaming hot tea. The mugs looked as though they hadn't been washed since they were new.

'Thank you,' said the Doctor.

'They're all talking about you lot in the dug-out,' said the sergeant. 'You'll see, in no time you'll all be interned somewhere safe.' He grinned and went back to making tea for himself and other soldiers.

The trio were squatting on slatted planks in the bottom of a deep trench. The walls of the trench were higher than a man, and the trench ran as far as the eye could see.

Jamie sipped his tea. 'Is this how they fought your First World War? Sitting in trenches?'

'The trench,' said the Doctor, 'was peculiar to that war. Before 1914 people charged about on horses, and armies took up positions and had set battles. This war was different. You see, they had invented the machine-gun but they hadn't developed the tank, not until towards the end.'

'I don't understand,' moaned Zoe. 'My clothes are filthy, I'm wet, it's uncomfortable, and I don't know what you're talking about.'

'Then I shall explain. Armies used to advance on each other. But once you have the machine-gun you can stop soldiers coming at you. You simply mow them down. The only way to advance on a machine-gun is with a tank. But they haven't got tanks yet. So both sides dug trenches. The trench we're in probably goes on for hundreds of kilometres, right across Europe.'

'That's a daft way to run a war,' said Jamie.

'It's more than daft,' the Doctor retorted. 'It was terrible. Every now and then one side or the other goes over the top. They climb out, hundreds of them, and go charging through No Man's Land towards the enemy's trenches. They know that the first wave will be wiped out by enemy machine-guns. The second wave, following immediately behind, will lose fifty per cent. With luck, some of the third wave will reach the enemy trenches while the machine-gunners are reloading. Once there, they kill every enemy soldier in sight and try to take the trench. An advance like that may push the front line forward by one kilometre at the cost of ten thousand soldiers' lives.'

Jamie and Zoe said nothing for a few moments. Then Jamie said, 'I asked you what that awful smell is, Doctor? You never answered.'

'That smell,' said the Doctor, 'is death. It's all around us. I told you, this is one of the most terrible times in history.' He put down his mug, the tea untouched. 'Anyway, I think the time has come for us to move on. If we leave here now we may be able to get back to the TARDIS before nightfall. You two stay where you are while I spy out the land.'

The Doctor rose and went to a crudely made ladder that stood propped against the side of the trench. Checking that the sergeant and his friends were busy making tea, he began to climb. As soon as he reached the top and put his head up over the edge of the trench, there was a burst of machine-gun fire. He ducked down.

'Hey, what d'you think you're doing?' The sergeant ran along the trench to the Doctor, grabbing his long black coat to pull him down.

'Nothing to worry about,' said the Doctor. 'We want to return to our transport now.'

'Really? And where's that?'

'Roughly,' said the Doctor, 'in the direction I was trying to go.'

'There's nothing in that direction except the Huns.' The sergeant stood between the Doctor and the ladder, barring further attempts to get away. 'Why should you want to get to the Germans?' All his previous friendliness had vanished.

Some of the soldiers had come forward to listen. 'Maybe he's a spy,' said one of them. 'All three of them are civilian spies. They should be shot.'

'I can assure you,' the Doctor insisted, 'we are not spies. We are travellers who just happened to arrive here.'

'They look like spies,' said a soldier. 'I've shot two spies before now, shot them in cold blood.'

'I think he's a rotten deserter,' said another soldier, pointing at Jamie. 'Look at his kilt. He's a deserter from a Highland regiment. All deserters should be shot.'

'This'll have to be reported,' said the sergeant. 'We caught you trying to make contact with the enemy.'

'This is nonsense,' the Doctor protested.

A small soldier, most of his head swathed in filthy bandages, pushed forward. 'With all my mates dead? With one of my ears half blown off? You call this nonsense? I say we shoot 'em now, Sarge.'

'There'll be none of that,' said the sergeant. 'They'll get a fair trial as German spies, and they'll be shot afterwards in the proper manner according to King's Regulations.'

A corporal ran down the trench towards the group. 'Sergeant,' he called as he neared the group. 'Major Barrington's decided what to do with this lot.' He indicated the Doctor and his friends. 'The Major's been on the blower to headquarters. General Smythe wants them all brought before him. He's going to have a full investigation made into what they're doing here.'

The sergeant grinned at the Doctor. 'You hear that? You're going up before General Smythe. And you know what we call him? The Butcher.'

*

The château, a once beautiful mansion belonging to a rich French family, was over thirty kilometres behind the front line. In the early part of the war, though, the château had been twice attacked and bitterly defended. One turret was missing, most of the three hundred windows were shattered, and two servants' cottages had received direct hits. Despite the damage it remained the most comfortable accommodation anywhere near the now static front line, and had therefore been commandeered by the British army as sectional headquarters.

General Smythe's office occupied what had been the main drawing room. Ornate chandeliers hung from the cracked, flaking ceiling. Heavy braided curtains were at the tall windows, many cracked or with the glass missing. All the original furniture had gone, burnt as firewood during the bitter winter of 1916. In its place were trestle tables and hardbacked chairs.

The general, a huge man with a square jaw and cheeks like cliffs, sat at one of the tables pondering over the telephone conversation he had just had. How could civilians possibly be in No Man's Land? It didn't make sense. Still, he would soon deal with them. His thoughts were interrupted by the arrival of his adjutant, Captain Ransom, who came in with his inevitable worried frown and file of papers.

'Sir,' said the captain. 'We are seriously short of men in the Number Three sector.'

'What?' The general had a way of pretending not to hear the first time. It put subordinates ill at ease.

The captain sat down at his trestle table desk, taking off his cap. He looked very tired. 'Last night's push over the top, sir. Number Three sector suffered seventy-five per cent losses.'

General Smythe scribbled a note on the back of an envelope. 'I've made a note. I'll get reinforcements as soon as possible.'

'Yes, sir.' It still appalled Captain Ransom that men's lives were reduced to reports and statistics, and notes on backs of envelopes. 'Do you realise, sir, we have lost twenty-nine thousand men in the past month?

It makes me wonder how long we can keep this up.'

General Smythe stood up to his full six feet. 'This is a war of attrition. If we can suffer our losses one day longer than the Germans can suffer their losses, we shall have won. By the way, some civilians found in No Man's Land are being brought here. I'm going to turn in for half an hour. Let me know when the civvies get here.'

'Yes, sir.'

Captain Ransom watched the general go into the little room he had chosen for a bedroom. It was said that the general never fully undressed and slept in his boots, always ready for action.

Smythe's little bedroom had once been a study. All the shelves were empty now. In a corner stood his camp bed, and in another corner a tall walnut wardrobe. Against one wall was a large steel safe that he always kept locked. The only decoration was a framed photograph of the British royal family.

General Smythe studied the photograph for a moment. Then he slid it to one side revealing the telecommunications unit set deep in the wall. He adjusted a control and a video screen lit up. The face on the screen was very familiar to him.

'What is it?' said the face.

'Smythe here,' said the general, though he knew that his fellow War Lord could see perfectly well who it was. 'This is the 1917 Zone, British area. We need reinforcements again.'

'How many?'

'About five thousand specimens.'

'It will be arranged,' said the voice. 'But we want to see you at Control in person.'

'Delighted,' said Smythe. 'I'll come right away.'

He turned off the video screen and replaced the portrait of the royal family. Then he went to the tall wardrobe, opened its doors and went inside.

*

Lieutenant Carstairs felt his luck was in to be driven away from the front line by such an attractive ambulance driver. Major Barrington, the front line commander, led the way in his staff car. He had invited Carstairs to be his passenger, but the young lieutenant said he thought that the ambulance should have his personal protection. What's more, the ambulance contained the three troublesome civilian prisoners and he did not want them to escape. They were safely in the back, guarded by four armed privates.

'My name is Carstairs,' he said when they were under way. 'Jeremy Carstairs.'

'Jennifer,' she responded. 'Actually. Lady Jennifer Buckingham.' She giggled.

'Good gracious, fancy you driving an ambulance.'

'Why not?' She changed gear as they went around a shell crater in the road. 'Everyone has to do their bit for the old country.'

'You must be related to Lord Buckingham.'

'My father,' she said. 'What about your family?'

'Oh, we're just very ordinary people,' he answered. In fact his father owned two factories in Yorkshire and a chain of shops, but in those days you did not admit to a Lady that your father was in commerce.

'Still,' she said, charitably, 'you're fighting for your King and that's all that matters. How long have you been at the front?'

'I've been out here ...' He hesitated. 'That's odd, I can't remember.' He quickly tried to change the subject. 'Whereabouts is your hospital?'

'Oh, it's ...' She trailed off, her eyes looking straight ahead to the back of Major Barrington's car. 'It's not very far away.'

'But where?' asked Carstairs.

'You'll think me potty, but I can't quite remember.'

He looked at her. 'Any more than I can remember how long I've been here.'

She smiled very prettily. 'Don't let it worry you. We're probably both suffering from a bit of shell shock.'

15

'Yes,' he agreed, uncertainly. 'I suppose we are ...'

Sergeant-Major Burns shouted the order: 'Left, right, left, right. Prisoners and escort halt!'

The Doctor, Jamie and Zoe were marched into Smythe's office and stood in line before a trestle table. Carstairs and Lady Jennifer followed and stood to one side. Major Barrington came forward to Captain Ransom.

'Prisoners from the front line for interrogation, sir.'

'I'll get the General.' Ransom got up and went to the door of the little makeshift bedroom. He tapped and called, 'Sir, the prisoners are here.' There was no answer and he tapped again: 'Sir?' He turned to Major Barrington. 'The General was working most of the night. He's probably taking a nap.'

Quietly Ransom opened the door and went inside. The room was empty. Since the single window was barred against intruders, and since he had been in the office from the time he saw the general go into his bedroom, he was very puzzled. He went back into the office.

'The general must have slipped out for a moment,' he said, trying to believe himself. 'The prisoners can be locked up until he is ready for them——'

The bedroom door opened quietly and General Smythe stepped out. 'These are the prisoners, are they?'

Captain Ransom swung round, astounded to see the general. 'I just looked in your room, sir. You weren't there.'

Smythe fixed Captain Ransom with cold, staring eyes. In a steady voice he said, 'You looked into my room and I was sleeping.'

Ransom's eyes were also staring as he said in a slow mechanical voice, 'I looked into your room, sir, and you were sleeping.'

'Good,' said the general. 'Then let us proceed with the court martial.'

The Doctor stepped forward. 'Court martial? We're

civilians and we've done nothing!'

'The prisoner get back into line,' shouted Sergeant-Major Burns, reinforcing his order by pushing the Doctor back.

The general sat down at the trestle table with Major Barrington and Captain Ransom on either side of him. 'The statements of Lieutenant Carstairs and Lady Jennifer are already in evidence——'

'Where?' the Doctor cut in. 'They haven't said anything yet.'

'The incidents in question,' said the general, 'were relayed to these headquarters over the field telephone by Major Barrington from the front line. Any further interruptions and you will be taken to the cells and tried in your absence.' He paused. 'The prisoners took over the ambulance in No Man's Land with the co-operation of German soldiers. Fortunately, it was re-captured by Lieutenant Carstairs and his patrol. While being held at a forward command position, one of the prisoners attempted to make for the enemy lines with whatever information he had gathered about our strength and movements.'

'None of that's true,' Zoe protested. 'You've twisted it all round.'

'Why is there no officer to defend us?' asked the Doctor. 'Isn't that usual at a court martial?'

'You are vocal enough to defend yourselves,' replied the general. 'Have you any questions to put to the witnesses?'

'I certainly have.' The Doctor turned to face Carstairs. 'When your men recaptured the ambulance, wasn't it clear we were all prisoners of the Germans?'

Lieutenant Carstairs looked confused. 'I suppose so ... It ... It was all very confused ...'

Trying to jog his memory, Jamie said, 'We were crouched in the back and a German was holding a gun on us!'

Carstairs seemed to find difficulty in speaking. 'I ... I didn't see in the back of the ambulance ... I saw you all come out of the back, that's all ...'

'Has the defence finished with the witnesses?' asked

17

the general. 'If so, the court will now consider its verdict.'

The Doctor protested again. 'I've hardly started!'

Sergeant-Major Burns came and stood directly in front of the Doctor. 'Any more noise out of you, mate, and I'll smash your teeth in! You're a dirty German spy.'

The general conducted a brief whispered conference with Major Barrington and Captain Ransom. Then he looked up.

'The unanimous verdict of this court is guilty.' He looked towards Jamie. 'It is clear that you have been misled by this man and that you are a deserter from a Highland regiment——'

'I've never been in any regiment,' Jamie shouted.

'You will therefore be returned to your regiment,' the general went on, 'where we hope you will redeem your honour by giving your life for your country.' He turned to Zoe. 'You are found guilty of espionage, but in view of your tender age punishment will not be too harsh. You will serve twenty years in a civilian prison.' His gaze moved to the Doctor. 'You are a disgrace to England——'

'I'm not from England,' the Doctor tried to say.

'While brave heroes are laying down their lives in thousands we have no place for people like you. The court's sentence on you is execution by firing squad, to be carried out immediately.'

2

Escape

'Do you have any final words to address to this world?' asked Captain Ransom.

'I certainly have,' said the Doctor. He stood tied to a post against a wall at the back of the château. 'I demand the right of appeal. I demand to see a lawyer I demand the help of a defending officer——'

'If you have nothing to say by way of apology for your crime,' Captain Ransom broke in, 'we shall proceed.' With no more ado he tied a blindfold across the Doctor's eyes and marched away from his protesting prisoner.

'You can't do this!' Zoe screamed from where she was held by a sentry. 'This is murder!'

Captain Ransom turned to her. 'War is murder.'

For a moment she felt he was speaking his own mind, was no longer a puppet of the strange General Smythe. 'You know this is all wrong,' she said, her voice as calm as she could make it. 'You know this is wrong.'

'I know . . .' The Captain faltered. He seemed about to say something else when a sergeant barked at him.

'Firing party ready, sir.'

Twelve armed soldiers had lined up. Captain Ransom looked at them, confusion in his eyes.

'Awaiting your command, sir,' said the sergeant. Ransom still seemed uncertain, so the sergeant reminded him why they were all there. 'Ready to execute the spy, sir.'

'Yes, of course,' said Captain Ransom. He cleared his throat. 'Take positions.' Six soldiers in the front row knelt down and aimed their rifles; the six soldiers behind raised their guns to fire from a standing position. 'Ready,' said Captain Ransom. 'Take aim——'

Before he could utter the word 'Fire!' a single shot broke the silence. One of the kneeling soldiers fell backwards. Zoe looked up at the trees. For a second she saw a tattered British army uniform, a grimy unshaven face and the glint of a rifle. Another shot rang out. The sentry holding her fell to the ground.

'German sniper!' shouted Ransom. 'Fire at will!'

Now all members of the execution squad knelt to take aim and fire into the tree. Zoe raced across the grass to Doctor Who. She started to untie his hands.

'What's happening?' he said. 'Get this stupid blindfold off me, whoever you are. I want to see what's happening.'

Zoe released his hands first. He dragged off the blindfold himself. 'Who are they shooting at?'

But she didn't answer. She had already formed a plan of escape in her mind and this was no time for discussions. Grabbing the Doctor's hand she tugged him with her into dense bushes.

Jamie banged with both fists on the door of his prison cell.

'Hey,' he shouted, 'if you're going to return me to a regiment I never belonged to, hurry up and return me! I don't want to stay in this filthy hole.'

The only item of furniture in the cell was a strawfilled palliasse. The small, heavily barred window was far too high for anyone but a giant to look out of.

Footsteps were coming along the corridor outside. He thumped on the door again. 'I wasn't to be put in a place like this,' he called. 'I was told to go and die for my country.'

A key turned in the lock. Jamie stood back, hoping his pleas had been heeded. The heavy door swung into the cell. Outside were two British soldiers struggling to subdue an English redcoat.

'You get in there,' one of the soldiers shouted. 'We've got no time for deserters here!'

The redcoat was thrown bodily into the cell. By the

time he had scrambled to his feet the door was closed.

'I'm no deserter,' the man started to say. Then he saw Jamie. He looked down at the kilt. 'A Highlander! Keep away from me, you barbarian.' The man cowered back into a corner.

Jamie could not believe his eyes. 'You're ... you're from my time.' The long red coat, with its blue cuffs and white trimmings, was all too familiar to a Scottish lad who had fought for the Young Pretender over two hundred years ago. 'How did you get here?'

'I got lost,' said the Englishman. 'I don't rightly remember.'

'Listen,' said Jamie, 'what year do you think it is?'

'Only a Scots barbarian wouldn't know what year it is,' said the redcoat snidely.

'All right,' said Jamie, 'what date is it?'

'I don't rightly know the exact day of the month,' said the redcoat, 'but any fool knows this is the year of 1745.'

The Doctor lay on his stomach in tall grass looking down at the valley below. 'They were going to send him to some regiment or other. How do you know he was sent to a military prison?'

'I heard one of the officers tell one of those sergeants,' said Zoe. 'Do you think that could be it?'

The only sign of life in the valley was a grey, sombre building with rows of tiny windows. The Doctor produced a telescope from one of the many pockets of his black jacket. He fixed it to his eye.

'We may have struck lucky,' he announced. 'It's surrounded by sentries.'

'That doesn't sound very lucky.'

'It's a first step,' he said, pocketing the telescope. 'You need to recognise your target before you can hope to hit it ...' He trailed off. His attention had been taken by a khaki military car coming along the road just below them.

'Quick,' said the Doctor, springing to his feet.

21

'We've got to stop that.'

'How?'

But the doctor was already racing down the slope of grass towards the road. By the time Zoe reached him he had signalled the car to stop and was talking in an imperious voice to the startled corporal driver.

'About time! Where have you been?' the Doctor demanded.

The driver looked at him blankly. 'Sir?'

'Don't argue. We're from the War Office. Take us to the military detention centre immediately.

The driver gulped. 'The prison, sir?'

'Come along, my dear.' The Doctor helped Zoe into the back seat. 'The lower orders have no idea of punctuality. We have to do all the thinking for them.'

The driver was still looking at the Doctor. 'I was sent to meet you, sir?'

'Of course you were,' said the Doctor. 'Any more lip from you, my man, and it'll be the cells with only bread and water for three months, followed by twenty lashes while you are tied to a gun wheel, and after that you will be posted to the front line.'

The corporal cringed. 'Yes, sir. I was sent to meet you.' He put the car into gear and drove forward along the winding road.

The Doctor looked sideways at Zoe and grinned.

Beneath the chandeliers and cracked ceiling, Captain Ransom and Lieutenant Carstairs stood poring over maps of the area. Ransom was a very worried man.

'We've searched everywhere around the château,' he said. 'Not a trace. General Smythe will be furious.'

'Incidentally,' asked Lady Jennifer, 'where is the general?'

'He's . . .' Ransom was always forgetting things these days. 'He's attending a conference at high command. Look, I'd better take a search party towards the German lines. That's where these spies will be making for.'

'And I had better return to my unit.' Carstairs reached for his cap.

'Must you? I would rather leave an officer in charge here.' Captain Ransom picked up his swagger cane. 'Be a good fellow and stay until I get back, will you? Perhaps you could telephone all command posts and tell them to be on the look out for these people.' He hurried out of the office, terrified of what General Smythe would say when he heard the news of the escapes.

'I wouldn't like to be in his shoes,' said Carstairs when Ransom had gone. 'Better the front line any time than be adjutant to a general.'

Lady Jennifer regarded Carstairs a few moments before saying what was on her mind. 'Didn't you think there was something strange about that court martial, Jeremy?'

'Oh, I don't know,' he said, cheerfully. 'I suppose military justice can be a bit rough, not like the Old Bailey.'

'How much do you know about General Smythe?' she asked.

He tried to remember. 'Can't say I'd heard of him till I arrived here. What are you getting at?'

'Things have started to come back to me,' she went on. 'I can remember joining the Volunteer Ambulance Drivers and coming out to France to drive ambulances. I remember driving through a forest, then all of a sudden I was in a strange mist or fog. After that I was in a field dressing station, tending some wounded soldiers. But where was I between that mist and the field dressing station?'

'The mist you mentioned . . .'

'Yes?'

Carstairs smiled. At last his memory seemed to be returning. 'I remember a mist, but I don't know when. Perhaps the Germans have invented a new type of poison gas, one that affects our minds.'

'Do you really believe that?' she asked. 'And do you believe that was a fair court martial?'

He looked worried. Then his face cleared. 'Good

gracious, the Captain asked me to telephone the command posts about those escapees. I'd better get on with it.'

He picked up a field telephone and cranked the handle to get attention. Jennifer watched him.

Colonel Gorton stood at his office window while an orderly poured his afternoon tea. His view was pleasant: lush green fields and beyond, swathes of long grass gently rising up one side of the valley. If he cared to look down at a more acute angle he could see the barbed wire entanglements of the detention centre's outer periphery, and even closer at hand the parade ground where prisoners carrying full packs were marched and drilled, usually at the double. But he preferred to look straight ahead at the pleasant French countryside that reminded him so much of his boyhood in ... Was it Wiltshire, Oxfordshire or Berkshire? He couldn't quite remember.

'Will that be all, sir?' asked the orderly.

'Yes, thank you.'

The man hobbled out. The domestic orderlies were all wounded soldiers. Gorton felt sorry for the man, who would never walk properly again. For his prisoners, though, he felt no sorrow or pity. They were all deserters or men who had refused an order to go over the top to charge at the enemy's machine-guns. He was proud that it was his job to make life as uncomfortable as possible for these cowards. The telephone broke into his thoughts.

'Gorton here,' he said.

'Sir,' said a sergeant's voice he knew well, 'there's a gentleman here from the War Office. He says he has to see you, sir.'

'He's made no appointment with me,' said Gorton. 'Are you sure he's from the War Office?'

The sergeant lowered his voice. 'He seems a very educated gentleman, sir. I didn't ask for his papers, sir.'

'You'd better send him in.' Gorton replaced the

telephone thoughtfully. It was unnerving to have an unexpected inspection, if an inspection was the purpose of the visit. Everything, so far as he knew, was in perfect order in the prison. There had been that little problem with the French deserter who insisted he had been fighting for Napoleon Bonaparte. The man was obviously mad and had been taken away to a hospital. Apart from that everything was running smoothly. Even so, it was irritating to have civilian officials suddenly arriving like this.

The orderly tapped and opened the door. 'Your visitors from the War Office, sir.'

The Doctor strode in, followed by Zoe. 'I am an inspector from the War Office,' the Doctor announced. 'This young lady is my secretary. I take it you were expecting me.'

Colonel Gorton was surprised by his visitors' appearance: the man wore an extravagant, long black jacket and the girl was wearing trousers. But what surprised him most was that they were both spattered and caked with mud.

'As a matter of fact I wasn't,' he replied. 'May I see your identification papers?'

'How dare you,' said the Doctor. 'You send no car to meet us, we have had to walk miles in the rain, and now you doubt my authority!'

The colonel wondered if there had been a message that he had not received. If the visitor was an inspector he did not wish to cause offence. He liked being in command of a prison and was secretly terrified of ever being sent to the front line.

'Would you care for some tea?' he asked.

'We have no time for tea,' the Doctor blustered. 'We want to inspect your security.'

'My security is second to none, sir. Take a look at this map.' Gorton led the Doctor to a wall map of the entire prison. 'We have barbed wire, concealed trip wires, everything to make escape completely impossible.'

The Doctor studied the map. 'Hm, not bad. Let me see your list of new arrivals.'

'That's always kept up to date.' Gorton went to a desk drawer. 'Here are the latest,' he said, offering the Doctor a list.

The Doctor ran his eye down the names. 'What's this one,' he said, ' "Scottish Highlander awaiting return to regiment"?'

'Exactly what it says, sir.'

'I wish to question this man.'

Gorton was amazed. 'Speak to a prisoner?'

'It is my duty to learn both sides of how this prison is run. Kindly have the man brought here immediately,' said the Doctor, adding, 'in chains if you think it necessary.'

Gorton picked up his desk telephone. 'With an escape-proof prison as I have here, sir, such barbarities as chaining prisoners are entirely unnecessary.' He spoke into the telephone. 'Sergeant, bring the Highland deserter to my office immediately.'

'Sir,' said the sergeant's voice, very subdued, 'he's just escaped.'

Gorton's knuckles went white as chalk as he clenched his fist. 'What?' He was aware of the War Office inspector looking at him. 'What did you say?'

'There was the two of them fighting in their cell, sir,' the sergeant replied. 'They were shouting about Scotland versus England or something. It sounded like they was going to murder each other. So two of my men barged in to quiet them. But it was a trick. They set on my men and both got out. We're hunting them down in the grounds now, sir.'

'Bring him to me as soon as you can.' Gorton cradled the phone.

'Some little problem?' asked the Doctor.

'He'll be here in a moment,' said Gorton. 'I could have another pot of tea brought in if you wish?'

From outside, came the sound of a volley of shots. Zoe ran to the window. 'What are those soldiers shooting at?'

'I imagine a little target practice,' said Gorton. 'My guards like to keep their hand in, in case they're ever needed at the front.'

'They've wounded someone,' Zoe exclaimed. 'They're carrying him.'

The Doctor rushed to the window and looked down. There was no one in sight now. 'Who was it?'

'He had a red coat.'

Colonel Gorton came to the window, pretending to share their interest. 'We get chaps in all sorts of uniforms here. From different regiments, don't you know. What about this spot of tea?'

'I want to know,' said the Doctor, 'what or who those soldiers were firing at.'

'I imagine I could find out ...' The colonel made a pretence of returning to his telephone, but before he had lifted it there was another tap on the door. It opened and two soldiers entered with Jamie.

'The Highlander, sir,' said one of the soldiers.

Jamie stared. 'Doctor!'

'Dismiss your guards,' the Doctor told Gorton. 'Get rid of them.'

'Dismiss,' said Colonel Gorton. The two soldiers hurried out.

'Doctor,' Jamie said, grinning, 'what are you doing here?'

The Doctor replied sharply to him. 'You speak when you're spoken to, my man.'

'Who's side are you on?' Jamie blurted, hurt by the Doctor's sharpness, 'I and another fellow had just escaped——'

'Escaped?' The Doctor swung round to Gorton. 'You didn't mention this. Is that what the shooting was about? And you claim this prison is not barbaric?'

'An escaping prisoner must expect to be shot at,' said Gorton. 'How is it this prisoner seems to know you, sir?'

'He's mistaken me for somebody else.'

'Are there many people dressed like you, I wonder?' Gorton put his hand on the telephone. 'By which military authority are you in the fighting zone, sir?'

'General Smythe,' the Doctor said emphatically. 'If you ask any more impertinent questions, I shall require to use your telephone to call him.'

27

'There will be no need,' said Gorton. 'I intend to call him myself right now.' He lifted the telephone.

'You did say we might have some tea?' said Zoe.

'What?' Gorton was surprised by the question, then remembered he was an officer and gentleman. 'I could not deny refreshments to a lady.'

'Thank you very much,' said Zoe. But before Gorton could carry out the request, Zoe quickly picked up the teapot and brought it down smartly on his head. He collapsed forward onto the desk, unconscious.

'I know you hate violence,' she said innocently to the Doctor. 'But it seemed the only way.'

'Well done,' said the Doctor. 'Now let's see if we can bluff our way out of here. Come on.'

He hurried to the door followed by his two companions. 'If we could get into this place, we can get out!' With a cheerful flourish he flung open the door.

Standing immediately outside was Captain Ransom, revolver in hand. Either side stood armed soldiers.

'Going somewhere?' Ransom enquired. 'Perhaps I can give you a lift.'

3

The Time Mist

'This time,' said Zoe, 'that awful general will sentence us all to death.'

Glumly she surveyed their dismal surroundings. The trio were back in the château locked in a basement room. A little light came through a grille set near the ceiling. The place smelled of damp and age.

'About this redcoat,' the Doctor said to Jamie. 'He really believed he was in 1745?'

Jamie had told the story once already. 'That's right, Doctor. He said he was fighting my lot, then all of a sudden he was in another war—this one. Do you think he was crazy?'

'No crazier than our so-called court martial. Anyway, I'm glad to know they only wounded him.' The Doctor looked around the basement room. 'How are we going to get out of here?'

Zoe had gone to the door. 'Shhh! I think someone's coming.'

'Right,' said the Doctor. 'You step aside, Zoe. Leave this to us.'

The Doctor and Jamie took up positions either side of the door. Listening intently they heard the footsteps of one person approaching. Jamie grinned; knocking out one man would be easy. A key turned in the lock and the door slowly opened. Jamie was about to deliver the first blow, but the Doctor had seen who it was.

'No, Jamie. I think this may be a friend.'

Lieutenant Carstairs came in quietly and closed the door behind him. He looked at each of the three prisoners yet said nothing.

'You wanted to see us?' the Doctor asked. 'I'm afraid we can't invite you to sit down.'

'Who are you people?' Carstairs asked.

The Doctor smiled. 'Are you sure that's what you really came to talk to us about, Lieutenant?'

'Perhaps not.' Carstairs hesitated. 'I don't understand what's going on any more.'

'It's pretty simple,' said Jamie. 'You've got this war on and you're all mad!'

'Just a moment, Jamie.' The Doctor turned back to the lieutenant. 'What do you know about General Smythe?'

Carstairs passed a hand over his forehead. 'That's the point. Lady Jennifer and I have been having a talk. She thinks that court martial wasn't at all fair.' Then he added with some pride, 'We're English, you know. We believe in playing cricket, doing the right thing.'

'Of course,' said the Doctor. 'But I want to take your mind back to something. You remember when Captain Ransom looked in that little room off the main office and couldn't find the general? Then a moment later the general emerged from that same room?'

'Yes,' said Carstairs. 'I think so ...'

The Doctor went on, 'The captain said, "I looked in your room, sir. You weren't there." General Smythe stared at the captain and said, "You looked into my room and I was sleeping." Do you recall that?'

'I do,' said Carstairs. 'It struck me as rather odd.'

'It was even more odd when Captain Ransom replied, "I looked into your room, sir, and you were sleeping." ' The Doctor paused to let that sink in. 'The general was telling the captain what he had to remember.'

Carstairs looked even more worried. 'Yes, memory ...'

'What about memory?' asked the Doctor.

'It all hinges on memory, don't you see? I can't remember things. Lady Jennifer says her memory is coming back, but not completely.' Carstairs tried to give a boyish grin. 'It's all so confusing.'

'Lieutenant,' said the Doctor. 'Would you allow us

to see into that other room? The one that the general came from?'

'It's his bedroom, I believe.'

'Whatever it's supposed to be,' the Doctor insisted, 'may we see inside it?'

They all looked at the young man, waiting for his answer.

'We won't run away,' Zoe promised. 'We want to help you.'

'You do promise not to escape again?' said Carstairs. 'It would be my duty to shoot you, including the young lady. Is that understood?'

'We give our solemn promise,' the Doctor assured him.

'Then wait here until I return.' Lieutenant Carstairs left the basement room as quietly as he had arrived. Jamie went forward to pull open the door just as they heard the key turn in the lock.

'I can't say my job here is particularly easy,' Captain Ransom was saying. He was sitting back, drinking a cup of tea that Lady Jennifer had made for them both. 'There's a dashed lot of paper work. Can you imagine, one of the forward posts lost a hundred and fifty shovels last week, couldn't account for them.'

'That must have been very annoying,' said Lady Jennifer. She had been listening to Ransom for the past half hour and was very bored. But she had promised Carstairs to keep him talking while the lieutenant made his secret visit to the prisoners.

'Jolly inefficient,' said Ransom. He checked his watch. 'Well, it's been nice talking, Lady Jennifer. I'd better rouse up another execution party. If that spy hasn't been shot dead by the time General Smythe returns, my life won't be worth living.' He laughed and picked up his cap.

'Must you go? I'd so much like to hear more about shovels and things.' Jennifer desperately tried to think of some way to keep him in the room.

'Well, as a matter of fact, there are some other interesting things I could tell you. For instance——'

To Jennifer's relief the phone rang. She picked it up.

'I'm on the basement extension,' Lieutenant Carstairs whispered. 'Now is the time to get Ransom out of the main office.'

'Why, certainly, General Smythe,' Jennifer said brightly. 'I'll tell him immediately.'

'Is that for me?' said Ransom, reaching for the phone.

'Oh, sorry.' She had replaced it on the cradle. 'How stupid of me not to let you speak to him. General Smythe wants you at number seventeen command post immediately.'

'Really? What's he doing there? It's the farthest end of the section.'

'It was not for me to ask,' said Jennifer. 'He sounded in a great hurry.'

Ransom considered. 'I'd better go and shoot the condemned man myself before I go.' He drew his revolver.

'Wouldn't that be against King's Regulations, a one-man firing squad?'

'I suppose you're right.' He holstered the gun. 'Don't you think it was a bright idea of mine, looking for them at the prison? I tried to think of the most unlikely place they would be, and there they were.'

'It was a brilliant stroke,' she agreed.

'Not exactly brilliant, ma'am. Just tried to use a bit of common sense.' He finished the remains of his tea. 'All right, off I go to number seventeen command post. Very nice talking with you.' He hurried out of the office.

As a precaution, Jennifer went to the shattered windows to watch Captain Ransom get into his car and drive away. When she was sure he had gone she returned to the telephone. She was about to pick it up as Carstairs entered with the Doctor, Jamie and Zoe. This was something she hadn't expected.

'Those people are prisoners,' she protested to Carstairs. 'We agreed you should go and talk to them, but not to release them.'

Carstairs went directly to the general's bedroom. 'It's all right. They won't run away.' He opened the door. 'Is this what you want to see?'

The Doctor went into the little room. 'Now, where could the General have been when Captain Ransom looked in here and didn't see him?'

'Out through this window,' said Jamie. He went up to the window and looked. 'No, it's got bars.'

'A trap door?' Zoe suggested. She looked at the floor.

'Some kind of invisible door in a wall?' said Carstairs. 'At music halls I've seen conjurors do all sorts of extraordinary tricks.'

'It's possible,' the Doctor said. He went along the walls tapping. As he came to the photograph of the Royal Family he pushed it to one side to see if anything was hidden behind it. 'Well, well, look at what we have here!'

'It's a video screen,' Zoe exclaimed. 'Did they have television in 1917?'

'No more than they had English redcoats,' the Doctor said. 'Lieutenant Carstairs, Lady Jennifer, take a look at this.'

The couple stared at the wall. 'Look at what?' Carstairs asked.

'That thing,' said Jamie. 'It's right before your eyes, man.'

Lady Jennifer was puzzled. 'What are we supposed to be looking at?'

'Concentrate,' the Doctor implored. 'Look at the wall and concentrate.'

'I'll try.' Jennifer narrowed her eyes. She gave a little start. 'My goodness, there's a sort of frame there, a blank picture. And what are these knobs?' Instinctively she reached forward and touched the 'on' control.

'I can see it too,' said Carstairs with astonishment. 'Not very clearly, but I can just see it in the wall. What's it for?'

'It's like a telephone,' Zoe explained, 'but one where people can see each other.'

'Then who's at the receiving end?' Carstairs asked.

'That's what we have to find out.' The Doctor noticed a small red light had started to glow. 'Good heavens, this thing is working.' He reached forward and touched the 'off' control.

'We didn't see anyone on the screen,' said Zoe.

'No, but someone may have seen us,' the Doctor said. 'Lieutenant Carstairs, Lady Jennifer, you must help us get away from here at once. And you must come too. All our lives may be in danger now.'

'You gave a promise,' Carstairs reminded the Doctor. 'You said you wouldn't run away.'

'He says we must go, too,' Jennifer reminded him. 'I think he's right. We must get away from this place and from General Smythe and ... and try to get our wits together.'

'What if we go to the Field-Marshal?' Carstairs suggested. 'Tell him everything.'

'Unless we leave quickly,' said the Doctor, 'we won't get to anyone.' He moved to the open door. 'I and my friends are going to leave now, Lieutenant. Will you shoot us down in cold blood?'

Once again the trio looked to Carstairs for his decision. It was taken by Lady Jennifer.

'I shall go with them,' she said. 'You'll have to shoot me, too.'

'It's all right,' said Carstairs. 'We'll all go together.'

Ten minutes after the group had left the bedroom, General Smythe's Space and Inter-time Directional Robot All-purpose Transporter, known by its initials SIDRAT re-materialised in the corner and resumed its appearance of a wardrobe. The general stepped out. He went straight to the photograph of the Royal Family, slid it to one side and checked that the controls of his telecommunications unit were correctly set. It was annoying that the Doctor had discovered so much, but there was little he could do to upset the plans of

34

the War Lords. Anyway, he and his friends would soon be dead. If the two humans who had seen the tele-communications unit survived they would be re-processed. General Smythe had been busy talking with his fellow War Lords when Lady Jennifer accident-ally turned on the video. Fortunately, another War Lord had spotted the monitor for the 1917 Zone be-come live. His description of the faces he saw staring into the screen told Smythe everything he needed to know.

Satisfied that the telecommunications unit had not been damaged, Smythe went into the main office. He was surprised to find Captain Ransom calmly reading a book.

'Oh, General,' said Ransom, springing to his feet. 'I didn't know you were back, sir.'

It crossed Smythe's mind that he should tell Ransom he had personally witnessed his return by motor car, and to get Ransom to repeat it. But he couldn't be bothered. More pressing matters were at hand.

'Why wasn't the spy shot?' he asked.

'The firing squad was sniped at,' said Ransom. 'It was all very confused. Still,' he added, trying to be cheerful, 'under the circumstances it's just as well the man's still alive.'

'Really? Why?'

'He's being taken to the Field-Marshal, sir.'

Smythe wondered if Ransom had gone quietly mad. 'Would you mind explaining what you're talking about, Ransom?'

Ransom gulped. 'First there was your phone call, sir, ordering me to meet you at number seventeen com-mand post.'

'*He's definitely gone mad,*' Smythe thought. He said, 'I told you to meet me?'

'Yes, sir. So I went there but I couldn't find you. On my return I arrived in time to find Lieutenant Carstairs and Lady Jennifer taking the prisoners to the Field-Marshal in accordance with your instruc-tions.'

'My instructions? What instructions?'

'The instructions you had given to Lieutenant Carstairs over the telephone while I was at number seventeen command post looking for you, sir.'

'You did nothing to stop Carstairs taking the prisoners away?'

'Well, I asked Carstairs if it was definitely your voice when he received the telephone call. He assured me that you had spoken to him personally, sir.'

'You have been tricked,' Smythe said. 'You are a fool.'

'Sir,' said Ransom, desperately trying to defend himself. 'Lieutenant Carstairs is a gentleman and a fellow officer. I had no reason to doubt his word.'

'Well, you have now. Every effort must be made, including heavy artillery, to stop the escaping party.'

Ransom was shocked. 'Fire on an ambulance, sir?'

Smythe stared straight into Ransom's eyes. 'They are all the enemy, Ransom. They must be killed.'

'Yes, sir.' Ransom's eyes were also staring now. 'They are all the enemy. They must be killed.'

From their hidden dug-out half-way up a peaceful hill, Willi Müller from Berlin and George Brown from London stared down at the ambulance and the shell explosions either side of the road. They had been in hiding three months, both having deserted their armies. They met by chance while wandering aimlessly in the woods, each expecting the other to kill him. But instead, the enemies had become friends and they intended to hide in their little dug-out until the war was over.

'Who would shell an ambulance?' said Willi.

'Not my side,' said George.

'Germans do not fire on ambulances,' said Willi. 'We are too far from the German lines. It *must* be your side.'

George was silent. What Willi said made sense. 'Anyway,' he said after a while, 'the ambulance is getting away, and good luck to them.'

They watched in silence for a couple of minutes as

the ambulance slowly drove along the valley. Then something happened that was beyond their understanding. George rubbed his eyes.

'What happened to it?'

'It's disappeared,' said Willi, incredulously. 'Before my eyes it vanished. I am looking, it is there, and then it is not there.'

''Struth,' said George. 'I wonder if we're both going barmy?'

'Barmy? What means barmy?'

'Out of our minds. Fancy seeing something vanish into thin air ...'

The ambulance had stopped. So had the shell explosions. In the back, the Doctor was poring over maps that Lieutenant Carstairs had taken from Smythe's headquarters before they made their escape.

'We don't seem to be moving,' said Jamie.

'What?' The Doctor had been too engrossed in the maps to notice. 'I wonder what's wrong?'

He got down onto the road and walked forward to the driving cabin. 'I say, are you two all right?' They had stopped in a woodland area. A thin mist drifted between the trees.

'I think this mist has affected Lady Jennifer,' Carstairs explained. He sat beside her in the passenger seat. 'Are you feeling a bit off?'

She held her hands to her head. 'I can't drive on. Something's ... stopping me.'

'Let me.' The Doctor scrambled up into the cab. 'May I take your place at the wheel?'

Without a word Jennifer moved over. The Doctor sat down, started the engine and drove forward.

'I feel rather odd, too,' Carstairs admitted. 'Doesn't this gas affect you?'

'It isn't gas,' said the Doctor. 'Anyway, it's clearing now. Look!'

They were almost out of the wood. Beyond was a peaceful country scene, and beyond that the sea and cliffs.

'We've reached the coast,' said Carstairs. 'I didn't realise we had come so far.'

'I think we've gone further than you imagine.' The Doctor continued driving a little way, then braked and turned off the engine. 'I want to get out and investigate.'

He got down from the cab and called to his friends. 'Zoe—Jamie! I'm going to take a little walk. Want to come?'

Zoe and Jamie climbed down from the rear of the ambulance. 'Where are we?' asked Jamie.

'I don't know, Jamie. But it looks different. It even smells different.'

Zoe looked around. 'There are no signs of that awful war.' The Doctor had already walked some distance from the ambulance and Zoe had to run to keep up. 'Where are you going?'

'No idea. I just feel there is something odd here and I want to know what it is.' The Doctor kept walking. 'You know, I think we have passed through some kind of force field.' He paused and breathed in the sweet country air. 'This is a very nice little valley.' He winked at Jamie. 'I wonder if we have somehow arrived in Scotland?'

'Don't pull my leg,' said Jamie. 'If we were in France ten minutes ago, we can't now be in ...'

He stopped, eyes on the hillside.

'Doctor,' he said, 'look!'

Racing down the hill towards them were two Roman chariots, knives sticking out from their wheels. Behind came a group of legionaries, shouting Roman war cries and raising their lances.

'Quick,' the Doctor shouted. 'Back to the ambulance!'

The three of them raced from the approaching Romans towards Carstairs and Jennifer, who were also staring in disbelief.

'Everyone get in,' the Doctor ordered. A thrown lance whipped over his shoulder and embedded itself in the ground. 'I'll drive,' he announced, scrambling behind the steering wheel. He started the engine, threw the gear into reverse and rammed his foot on the accelerator.

Drusus Gracchus of Rome pulled on his horses' reins, blinked and looked again. He called to his friend, Brutus Sullas, in the other chariot.

'The square elephant has vanished, Brutus,' he said, speaking Latin and trying to make sense of the ambulance's sudden and complete disappearance. 'It is an omen.'

'It was some Gaulish trick,' said Brutus, who tried to think scientifically.

'Such talk is dangerous,' said Drusus, who did not want his friend to get into trouble. 'It was an omen, a message from the God of War. We must make sacrifices to appease Mars.'

'If you insist,' said Brutus.

Drusus was glad his friend had seen reason. He turned his chariot round to head back to the fort. To-night he would sacrifice three goats, two pigs and a human slave to make the God of War happy.

4

Back to the Château

A distant rumble of heavy gunfire filled the air, yet where the ambulance stood all was peaceful. Shell craters pitted the land, but they were mainly water-logged and the shells had fallen some time ago. There was no sign of life except for the five wanderers who were now studying the maps.

'Are these the only maps you are given?' the Doctor asked.

'Yes,' said Carstairs. 'These are the regular issue.'

'I don't think they're much help. What we need is a map that shows all the time zones.'

'Time zones?' said Lady Jennifer.

'We went through that mist,' the Doctor said patiently, 'then we saw Romans. Don't you see, we went back two thousand years.'

'Of course,' Zoe exclaimed. 'We were following this road'—she pointed to the map—'and as soon as we went off the edge of the paper we were into another time.'

'People can't move through time,' Lady Jennifer protested. 'That's ridiculous.'

'No more ridiculous than me being in a prison cell with a stupid Sassenach from 1745!' Jamie said.

'Well,' said the Doctor, 'let's not argue among our-selves. What we need is a bigger and better map. I think I know where we can get one.'

'Where?' asked Carstairs.

'From General Smythe. We must return to the château.'

'After all that's happened?' said Lady Jennifer. 'How can we go back there?'

40

'Quite simple,' the Doctor answered. 'You're going to take us.'

Captain Ransom trimmed the wick of the oil lamp over his desk. It puzzled him how the ambulance had vanished without trace. After the general gave his order, a Sopwith Camel pilot had spotted the ambulance travelling through a valley. Fortunately, the plane was equipped with one of the new-fangled wirelesses; using Morse Code the pilot had told the heavy artillery gunner where to aim. Over two hundred shells were fired, enough to destroy an entire village. Yet when a ground patrol went to search for the wreckage of the vehicle, not a trace of the ambulance and its occupants was found.

Satisfied that the wick was now giving the best light possible, Ransom hung up the oil lamp and went back to his book. Before finding his place he glanced up at the chandeliers, trying to imagine what the château's main living room had been like when it was ablaze with light and in its former glory. Peace, he thought, must have been wonderful. The pity was, he could not remember what he had been doing before 1914, nor where he had been.

A motor vehicle pulled up outside. Quickly he put the book away. General Smythe had already caught him reading a book once; that was no way to get promotion. He brought out a work file on the supply and distribution of latrine buckets, spread papers all over his desk, and tried to give the impression of a man engrossed with his job. To his surprise, though, it was not the general who entered. It was the Doctor and Jamie, followed by Lieutenant Carstairs holding his gun on them.

'Reporting back, sir,' said the lieutenant. 'Returning the prisoners.' He barked at the Doctor, 'Keep still. One move from you and I fire.'

Ransom half rose in amazement. 'Carstairs, what on earth have you been up to? And why did you give me

41

that fake message from the general? You are in very serious trouble and you will be reported ...'

He went no further. Carstairs's gun was now pointing directly at his chest.

'Carstairs, are you out of your mind? Point the gun at the prisoners, not at me.'

'Sorry about this, sir,' Carstairs replied. He turned to Jamie. 'Get the Captain's revolver. Please don't do anything foolish, sir. Doctor, the bandages.'

While Jamie unholstered Ransom's service revolver, the Doctor produced rolls of bandages from his pockets.

'We're going to tie you up,' he explained. 'Before we gag you, would you care to tell us where the General keeps his maps?'

'You're a German spy,' said Ransom. 'I shall tell you nothing. As for you, Carstairs, you'll be court martialled for mutiny.'

'Why not leave him with me a few minutes, I'll get him to tell us everything,' Jamie suggested.

The Doctor shot him a withering look. 'Really, Jamie, we don't do that sort of thing. All right, Captain, hands behind your back, please.'

Within thirty seconds the captain's wrists and ankles were tied in bandages, his mouth gagged sufficiently to keep him quiet without causing suffocation. Carstairs dragged him to a dark corner of the office.

'I'm really very sorry, sir,' he said to the mute figure. 'But I believe this is for the best.'

The Doctor was already trying to pick the lock of the steel safe when Carstairs joined him in the general's bedroom. The Doctor was using a piece of wire that he had produced from his voluminous pockets.

'You'll get nowhere with that wee piece of wire,' said Jamie. 'It keeps bending.'

The Doctor straightened up. 'You're right. Lieutenant, since this is a military establishment, could you lay your hands on any explosives?'

'I could try,' said the lieutenant. 'Let me hunt around.' He hurried from the room. When Carstairs had gone, Jamie told the Doctor what was on his mind.

'Doctor, this is a terrible war and a terrible place

to be. Why don't the three of us try to get back to the TARDIS and leave them all to it?'

'Are you afraid, Jamie?'

'Och away, no,' Jamie said, trying to hide his nervousness. 'But it's such a miserable place.'

'I believe something very evil is going on here, Jamie. Not just this war. In any case, we now know there is more than one war—the British against the Germans in about 1917, the English against your people in 1745, even the Romans fighting two thousand years ago. How have all these soldiers been brought here and yet kept in their different time zones? And why? We can't run away without discovering what's behind all this.'

Jamie smiled. 'You never do run away, Doctor. You always want to put things right.'

'I am of an interfering nature,' the Doctor agreed amiably. 'Mind you, I'm not supposed to interfere.'

'Who says you shouldn't?'

'Well,' the Doctor said mysteriously, 'perhaps I may tell you one day.'

'And at this rate, perhaps we'll all be shot dead. Tell me now, who says you mustn't interfere. I thought you were your own master?'

'But I am,' the Doctor said. He turned back to the safe and tried again with his piece of wire. 'You'd think the lieutenant would have found some explosives by this time ...'

'Doctor,' Jamie persisted. 'You were going to tell me something about yourself. Who are you really? Where do you come from?'

'Another time, Jamie.' The Doctor turned the wire. 'I've almost got it ...'

'It's bent again,' said Jamie, exasperated. 'Aren't you going to tell me—please?'

The Doctor turned and looked at him. 'We've travelled together a long time, Jamie, so perhaps I should let you know who I really am. You see——'

Lieutenant Carstairs hurried back into the room. 'I've found this.' He held up a small metal object shaped like a pineapple. 'It's a Mills Bomb. I thought

43

we could hang it on the front of the safe and let it off.'

The Doctor took the bomb and examined it. 'That would blow up the room and might not harm the safe at all. We need to concentrate the explosion in the lock itself. If I remove the charge from this bomb ...'

'For goodness' sake be careful,' Carstairs warned. 'There's amytol in there.'

'That's a start!' The Doctor had managed to remove the pencil-shaped detonator and held it up for the others to see. 'Now all I have to do is to open the casing.' He fished in his pockets and brought out his sonic screwdriver. 'Lieutenant, do you mind looking the other way?'

'Why?'

'Because I've asked you. I can't think of any other good reason.'

'If you insist.' The lieutenant turned round.

Only a few seconds went by before the Doctor said, 'Bomb now open. Jamie, will you get me a sheet of paper from the other room. Anything will do.'

Jamie left the bedroom.

Carstairs looked at the two sections of bomb casing that the Doctor was holding. 'How did you open that?'

'It's not difficult when you have the knack.' The Doctor looked up, pleased to see Jamie back with a sheet of paper. 'Thank you. Now, this is what we do.'

Carefully he scraped the amytol onto the paper. Then he partly folded the paper into a channel so that the amytol could be guided down into the lock of the safe. 'All we need now is a fuse that will burn long enough to let us get out of this room before the explosion. Jamie, I think I noticed some candles in the other room.'

'Right, Doctor.' Jamie was already on his way.

Carstairs said, 'I would like to know why I had to turn away.'

'Afterwards,' said the Doctor. 'Let's first see if all this works. And if there is anything in the safe once we have opened it.'

*

44

'Shouldn't we go and see if they're all right?' said Lady Jennifer. She was huddled in a corner in the back of the ambulance. It was pitch dark now.

'The Doctor told us to wait here,' said Zoe. 'He knows what he's doing.'

'Where did the three of you meet up?'

'We just met.'

Zoe expected Lady Jennifer to pursue the question. But Jennifer had other things on her mind. 'I wish this war would end.'

'By your side killing more of the other side?' said Zoe.

'No. I used to think war was rather a lark. Now I've seen it, it's a different matter.'

'Perhaps if women took over we wouldn't have wars,' Zoe suggested.

'That's radical talk. A woman's place is in the home.' Lady Jennifer realised what she had just said. 'Except, of course, during a war.'

'Which men have started,' said Zoe.

'You're not one of these new socialists, are you?'

'I don't know,' Zoe replied honestly. 'What are they?'

'They believe in a lot of nonsense——'

Any further discussion was cut short by a violent explosion somewhere inside the château. It was followed immediately by the shouts of guards calling orders to each other. Lady Jennifer crawled to the rear of the ambulance and pushed open the door. She saw flashlights as guards ran about in confusion.

'Well, that's that,' she said flatly. 'Someone must have thrown a handbomb at them.'

'A handbomb?'

'It's made to fragment. Horrible wounds. I think we had better prepare ourselves for recapture. I shall be sent home in disgrace,' said Lady Jennifer in despair. 'And you will have to serve your twenty years.' She pushed the door wide open. 'I'll call to the guards and we can give ourselves up.'

'We'll do no such thing!' replied Zoe indignantly.

'It will be for the best, my dear. I can hear men

45

running towards us now. They must know all about us——'

The running men reached the ambulance. Jamie scrambled into the back clutching a sheaf of maps.

'It's me,' he called in the darkness. 'We've got what we wanted!'

As he spoke the engine started. The Doctor, with Carstairs beside him, drove away from the château at breakneck speed.

It was dawn. After driving much of the night, pausing only a short time to sleep, the group now sat in the back of the ambulance studying the maps found in General Smythe's safe. The largest map was spread out on the floor.

'Just as I suspected,' said the Doctor. 'The whole area is divided into time zones.'

The map, which showed roads, rivers and hill contours, was segmented by straight black lines. In each zone was printed a date in large black numbers—1862, 1951, 1776, 1917. Some zones carried the names of warring periods—Punic Wars, Mongol Invasion. A small area in the centre of the map was completely blank.

'Where do you think that is?' Zoe asked, pointing. 'It hasn't even been printed on.'

'Exactly,' said the Doctor. 'I think that's where we must make for.'

'I find this most difficult to understand,' said Carstairs. 'All these wars are going on at the same time?'

The Doctor nodded. 'For some reason that we don't understand—yes. My guess is that whenever we come to these dividing lines we'll find that mist ...' He stopped, listened, and put his fingers to his lips. They all stayed quiet as he crawled to the partly open rear door.

They had stopped the ambulance once again in No Man's Land. The Doctor saw the spike of a German helmet bobbing up and down behind a mound of mud. He looked around and saw two more. He retreated back into the ambulance.

'We've been found, I'm afraid. We're probably already surrounded. Lieutenant, lie down on a stretcher and pretend to be wounded. And you, Lady Jennifer, look after him. Zoe and Jamie, follow me.'

The Doctor slipped down onto the muddy road and made casually for the driving cabin. His companions came behind him.

'We'd better try to get started again,' he said, loud enough for the Germans to hear. 'That poor man must get to a hospital.'

The Germans waited until the Doctor had mounted the running board and was about to get behind the wheel. Then they emerged from shell holes all around, a morning patrol of about twenty men. Three came towards the Doctor.

'*Sie müssen mit uns kommen,*' one of them called.

'Come with you?' the Doctor called back. 'Yes, if you insist. Which way this time?'

While Carstairs lay moaning in the captured ambulance, tended by Lady Jennifer, and Jamie and Zoe sat in a German front line trench drinking coffee with some friendly soldiers, the Doctor was in a dug-out being questioned by Leutnant Lücke. Lücke was a stern, humourless young Prussian who tried to conceal his youth with a stiff military façade.

'For the last time,' he said in excellent English, 'what were you doing behind our lines?'

'I've told you,' said the Doctor. 'We were lost and the nurse gave us a lift.'

'Then what was *she* doing behind German lines?'

'She was lost, too. I do assure you, sir, we are quite harmless. That young officer is badly wounded, you know.'

'A doctor is on the way,' said Lücke. 'The British officer will be given our best medical treatment and sent to a prisoner of war camp. The nurse will be interned.'

'Thank you,' said the Doctor. 'That puts my mind

47

at rest. Well, I had better get on my way.' He rose to his feet.

Lücke smartly stepped between the Doctor and the exit to the trench. 'You are not going anywhere! Three people in civilian clothes behind our lines, that is very suspicious. Admit you are spies.'

'I can assure you we are not.'

'Then tell me where you came from *before* the British ambulance gave you a lift. And this time,' said Lücke, drawing his hand gun, 'I want the whole truth.'

The Doctor looked at the gun. 'Would you really shoot me? In cold blood?' He looked straight into the young officer's eyes. 'Could you kill a man you had been talking to?'

'You are appealing to my sense of decency,' Lücke said. 'All right, I won't point my gun at you.' He laid it on the crudely-made table, though he still kept his hand on it. 'Just remember thousands of German soldiers are giving their lives for the Fatherland every day, so military justice is sometimes rough. Now tell me the whole truth about yourself and your companions.'

'All right,' said the Doctor. 'But it will astound you.'

The young officer listened quietly while the Doctor explained truthfully that he was not of this planet, that Jamie came from 1745 and that he had met Zoe in a floating space station in the distant future.

'And that's where you all come from?' Lücke said scornfully when the Doctor had finished.

'I told you you would be astounded,' the Doctor answered. 'Ask my friends if you don't believe me.'

'I certainly shall!' Lücke turned towards the exit of the dug-out and shouted, *'Bringen Sie die anderen Engländer hierin! Sofort!'* He swung back to the Doctor. 'We shall soon see if your stories are the same.'

Zoe and Jamie appeared, behind them a soldier. Lücke waved the soldier away. 'Young woman, where did you meet this man?'

Zoe looked at the Doctor.

'I have told the whole truth, Zoe. You do the same.'

48

'We met in a space station,' she said.

'Really?' Obviously Lücke thought it was all nonsense. 'And you, Scotlander, where did you meet this man?'

'In Scotland.'

'When?'

'In 1745. We were fighting the English.'

Lücke seemed about to explode. 'This ambulance,' he shouted at the Doctor, 'it was going to a hospital or a lunatic asylum?'

The Doctor felt in his pockets and produced his sonic screwdriver. 'Where can I find a screw?' The crude table had been nailed together as had the simple wooden bed.

'What are you talking about?' Lücke demanded, losing his patience.

'I want to give you proof that I am not of this planet, nor of this time.' The Doctor noticed the gun. 'Ah, this will do nicely.'

Lücke's hand closed more firmly over the gun lying on the table, but the butt remained protruding. 'Don't you try to take my gun!'

'I have no such intention. But watch this.' The Doctor held his sonic screwdriver a couple of millimetres above one of the screws in the gun's butt. The screw began to turn and rise up on its own.

'You're using magnetism,' said Lücke, though the Doctor guessed he was curious and impressed.

'No, sir. I wasn't even turning the screwdriver. Now I'll make the screw go back.'

The screw wound itself back into the butt.

'But you did not touch the screw,' Lücke said. 'This is fantastic——'

'*Leutnant Lücke!*' A monocled German major had entered the dug-out.

Lücke sprang to attention. '*Major von Weich!*'

Major von Weich looked at the three strangers. '*Wer sind diese Leute? Was ist hier los?*' His voice was cold and menacing. ('Who are these people? What is going on here?')

Lücke remained at attention. '*Das sie die englischen*

49

Zivilisten.' ('These are the English civilians.')

Von Weich looked at the Doctor. 'What are you doing here? Where do you come from?'

Lücke answered for the Doctor. *'Er hat mir gesagt, dass er aus einem anderen Zeitalter in etwas namens TARDIS kommt.'*

'Time travellers?' said Major von Weich. 'In something named TARDIS?'

The Doctor began to say, 'I know this is difficult to believe . . .'

But Major von Weich was not listening. He had turned back to Leutnant Lücke and had fixed him with a steady stare. *'Es sind englische Spione. Wir müssen sie festhalten. Ich werde mit dem General darüber sprechen.'* ('They are English spies. We must hold them. I shall go and speak with the General.')

Lücke responded in a trance-like state. *'Jawohl, Major von Weich. Es sind englische Spione.'*

Von Weich stepped out of the dug-out. Jamie couldn't contain himself. 'They're talking to each other just like those two officers were before our court martial!'

'Listen,' the Doctor implored. 'We are not spies. We are from another time.'

'You are spies,' said Leutnant Lücke icily. 'In accordance with the rules of war, which Germany strictly observes, you will be shot!'

In another dug-out a few metres further along the trench, Major von Weich stood before a framed photograph of Kaiser Wilhelm, Emperor of Germany. He slid aside the photograph to reveal a telecommunications unit. He activated the 'on' control and waited for the video screen to come to life before speaking.

'Von Weich, 1917 German Front Line to Central Control. We have captured the three people who escaped from the British sector. I await instructions.'

The face of General Smythe looked at him from the screen. 'Kill them immediately, please.'

5

The War Room

'Before that major came in,' Zoe said indignantly, 'you were ready to believe us.'

'He hypnotised you,' Jamie said. 'That's what they call it.'

'Don't you remember my special screwdriver?' asked the Doctor.

Lücke was struggling, obviously confused. 'Please, don't all talk at once.' He waited for silence. 'Yes ... you did something with the gun.'

'Put your gun back on the table and I'll do it again.'

Lücke had holstered his Luger. He looked from one to the other suspecting a trick.

'Keep your hand on it if you wish,' the Doctor said. He got out his screwdriver again.

Cautiously Lücke placed the gun back on the table, his hand firmly on the barrel. The Doctor repeated the demonstration. Memory returned to the German's troubled face.

'Yes, I remember. But how is it possible?' In his confused state, Lücke lifted his hand from the gun.

'We have more tricks than that,' the Doctor said. 'Let me show you.' He picked up the gun and threw it to Jamie. 'Catch!'

Jamie neatly caught the gun and pointed it at the Leutnant. 'That's our best trick of all.'

'Now, Leutnant Lücke,' the Doctor said, putting his arm around the officer's shoulder, 'perhaps you would be good enough to take us back to our ambulance.'

'For losing my gun,' said Lücke, his face sombre, 'I shall be court-martialled.'

'Then be glad you're on the German side,' said Zoe. 'We've had a British court martial, and they're awful!'

*

General Smythe and Count Vladimir Chainikof stood together by a huge illuminated map in the centre of the war room. Black uniformed technicians at the far side were dealing with calls from the many time zones, coming in on the telecommunications central control.

'Well,' said Chainikof, 'and how is your war going?'

'Enormous losses,' said General Smythe. 'That's why I'm here again, to ask for new specimens. What about you?'

Chainikof wore the long grey topcoat and tall leather hat of a Russian officer in the Crimean War. 'My soldiers are illiterate peasants. But the survivors are good fierce warriors. They will be useful when the time comes to fulfil our destiny.' He gave a little laugh. 'Incidentally, we are fighting the British!'

General Smythe laughed too. 'Perhaps we should not be talking to each other!' He saw that Chainikof wanted to go. 'It was good seeing you again.'

Chainikof nodded farewell and strode towards the sidrat materialisation area.

Smythe called to a technician. 'When is the War Chief due back?'

'Now,' the technician replied. 'He's just returned from our planet.'

At the far end of the room double doors opened. All the technicians turned to bow as the War Chief entered with his personal armed bodyguard. He was a tall man, resplendent in his uniform of black with gold and red piping. He acknowledged the silent greeting, noticed General Smythe and walked towards him.

'I hear you lost your three civilian prisoners. How was that?'

'They have been recaptured, sir,' said the general, 'in the German sector. They will be shot immediately.' He tried to make light of his mistake. 'They keep telling a ridiculous story that they are time travellers!'

The War Chief did not share the general's amusement. 'Time travellers? And you ordered them to be killed?'

'Whatever they are,' the general blustered, 'they are no use to our plans——'

52

'Think,' said the War Chief, cutting in. 'If we did not bring them here, how have they arrived? I want them brought to me for interrogation.'

'I shall arrange that immediately,' said General Smythe. He hurried to the telecommunications central control. To his surprise, a technician was beckoning to him and von Weich's face was on one of the many screens.

'Those prisoners,' said von Weich, 'they tricked my human subordinate. They are probably on their way back to your lines.'

The War Chief had joined General Smythe at the video screen. 'Issue a general alert to all time zones,' he announced. 'I want these people captured alive. Officers are to describe this ambulance to their human troops as a hostile vehicle that must be stopped.'

General Smythe stood to attention. 'I shall issue the alert personally, sir. Excuse me.' He pushed a technician out of the way to get to one of the telecommunication video units.

The War Chief wandered back to the centre of the room and stood staring down at the war map. 'Time travellers?' he murmured to himself. 'I wonder ...'

'That's interesting,' said Lady Jennifer. 'I hardly felt that mist at all.'

The ambulance was going along a rough road in lush green countryside, Jennifer driving again and Carstairs beside her. To their left the grass on a gentle hill looked almost blue. Grazing deer scuttled out of the way at the sound of the motor.

'Stop a moment,' said Carstairs. 'I had better tell the Doctor.'

As Jennifer slowed and stopped, Carstairs jumped down and ran round to the back of the ambulance. 'We've just been through another of those mists, Doctor.'

The Doctor looked at the map they had acquired from General Smythe's safe. 'I calculate we are here,' he said, pointing. 'America in 1862.'

'What was happening then?' Zoe asked.

'The American Civil War,' replied the Doctor. 'Or some called it the War Between the States.'

'Anyway, it's another war,' said Jamie.

The Doctor pointed to the map again. 'If we are still on the right road, this is leading us direct to the blank area in the middle of the map——'

A shot rang out. Carstairs saw a soldier in light grey uniform pop behind a tree. He drew Leutnant Lücke's Luger, which he had thrust under his belt.

'Let's just keep going,' the Doctor said. 'These people used muzzle-loaded guns. It'll be another twenty seconds before that sniper can fire again.'

'I think you're right.' Lieutenant Carstairs ran back to the driving cabin. As he mounted the running board Jennifer let in the clutch. They were under way again.

Behind the tree, Private Cornelius Lanier of the 2nd Virginia Battalion hurried to re-load his rifle. He had put the powder in the breech and now dropped down the long muzzle the little metal ball that was a bullet. He looked around the tree to fire again. To his annoyance the Yankee covered wagon was already too far down the road for him to hit it. Resigned, he decided to wait with his loaded gun for any more Northerners that might come by.

The winding road narrowed between high trees and turned a bend. Lady Jennifer had slowed the ambulance to a few kilometres per hour. As she turned the bend the fallen tree came into sight. There was no room to turn back. She braked hard. Lieutenant Carstairs ran forward to inspect the tree. It had been freshly sawn through at the base.

'Jamie,' he shouted. 'We have to move this.' He looked around nervously, almost expecting an ambush.

Jamie came running from the back of the ambulance. 'That should give the two of us no trouble,' he said cheerfully. He took a second look at the size of the tree. 'Well, not if we all help. Doctor! Zoe!'

The Doctor and Zoe came forward. Carstairs had both his guns drawn.

'I suspect there may be snipers in the trees,' he whispered. 'You three do what you can with the tree while I cover you.'

Without a word they struggled to lift one end of the tree and wheel it round parallel with the road. Two shots rang out from hidden snipers and the trio immediately flattened onto the road. Carstairs crouched and fired at where he thought the shots came from.

'Quickly,' said the Doctor. 'Remember, they have to re-load.'

Fear gave them extra strength. Pulling and pushing one end of the tree they moved it enough to give the ambulance clearance. At once Lady Jennifer began to move forward.

'Jump on the running-boards!' she shouted as the ambulance lumbered towards them.

A volley of shots came from the trees, more than two this time. While the Doctor, Jamie and Zoe scrambled onto the moving ambulance, Carstairs stood his ground giving return fire.

'Lieutenant,' the Doctor called, 'climb on board!'

The cab passed Carstairs as he continued to fire into the trees. The Doctor reached out to help him onto the running-board but Carstairs ignored the helping hand.

'For goodness' sake,' the Doctor shouted, 'scramble into the back!'

The Doctor leaned out from the running-board to look to the rear. Having emptied both guns, Carstairs was running to get into the back of the ambulance as Confederate horsemen bore down on him from either side of the road, cutting him off from the ambulance. One struck a blow with his fist and Carstairs sprawled across the little narrow road.

'What shall I do?' asked Lady Jennifer, who had seen Carstairs fall in her rear mirror.

'Accelerate,' said the Doctor. 'It's the only thing we can do.'

Ashen-faced. Lady Jennifer put her foot down on the accelerator. The ambulance careened forward, swaying wildly on the unmade road.

Jamie was now looking behind. 'They've got him and they're coming after us!'

A bullet whizzed by the cab. They heard the shot a moment afterwards.

'Can this outpace a horse?' asked the Doctor.

'On a proper road it will,' said Lady Jennifer, working the steering wheel to save them crashing into the trees. 'Not on a track like this.' She saw another bend in the road. 'This might help us ...'

She swung round the bend. Temporarily, the pursuing horsemen were lost from view in her rear mirror. Just after the bend an even, narrow road branched off to the right. Making rapid gear changes, braking hard, she swung the ambulance right into the smaller road. It was full of gaping pot holes.

'You've tricked them!' Jamie yelled. 'They've kept going.' He looked with delight at the Confederate horsemen galloping along the road they had just left. 'You've fooled them——'

The ambulance lurched to a stop with a thunderous crack. The rear end sagged dangerously to one side. Lady Jennifer quietly turned off the motor.

'I'd say that's the back axle gone, wouldn't you, Doctor?'

The Doctor stepped down, looked under the ambulance, then straightened up. 'We'll have to press on by foot.'

'What about Lieutenant Carstairs?' asked Zoe.

'He did what was expected of an officer and a gentleman,' said Lady Jennifer, allowing herself no outward signs of emotion. 'Shall we continue the journey?'

Without waiting for their reply she turned and walked ahead. 'Has she no human feelings?' said Jamie, obviously astounded by Lady Jennifer's behaviour.

'She's an English aristocrat,' the Doctor explained quietly. 'When it come to being brave, you can't beat them. I suggest we follow.'

56

The Doctor returned to the back of the ambulance to collect his maps. Then he trudged after Lady Jennifer, and Jamie and Zoe trailed behind.

The great house, built all of wood in the American style, was completely gutted by fire, its once proud veranda pillars were now charred stubbs. But the near-by barn was intact, deserted, and very inviting to the four weary travellers. Jamie looked inside at the bales of straw.

'This'll do for the night, Doctor. I'm whacked!'

Jamie went forward and sprawled onto a bed of hay. The others followed inside and looked around.

'Are we still headed in the direction you wanted?' Lady Jennifer sat down on a bale of straw. She looked totally exhausted but was too well-bred to lie full out like Jamie.

'Yes,' the Doctor assured her. 'I've kept my eye on the map. We're on an almost straight line towards that blank centre in the middle. Lady Jennifer?'

But Her Ladyship had keeled over and was fast asleep. The Doctor and Zoe sat down.

'What's this war about?' Zoe asked.

'It started in 1861 and went on for three terrible years,' said the Doctor. 'The Southern states had Negro slaves. In the Northern states, owning slaves was out-lawed. The North wanted the South to free its slaves, so the Southern states tried to leave the Union ...'

He looked at Zoe. She too had fallen asleep. Coming from the distant future, she hadn't even heard of the United States.

The Doctor settled back to rest after the long walk. He was about to doze when he noticed three or four horse saddles hanging from pegs along one wall. The burnt out house had suggested the entire place was deserted. But would such costly objects as saddles still be there if no one ever used the barn now?

It was as this thought crossed his mind that he heard the noise, a wheezing sound like trumpeting elephants. In seconds it increased in volume. Jamie sprang up.

'What's that?' He looked puzzled. 'It's ... it's the sound of the TARDIS, Doctor!'

The Doctor shook Zoe and Lady Jennifer. 'Quickly, we must hide,' he shouted above the sound. 'Behind these bales.'

The barn was filled with the noise by the time the group had concealed themselves. Lady Jennifer, who had never heard such a sound before, shouted out to ask what it was, but Jamie put his hand over her mouth to silence her.

The sidrat materialised in the centre of the barn, a tall black box similar in shape and size to the TARDIS. Once it was fully visible the sound ceased. Slowly a door opened. To everyone's amazement fresh-faced young soldiers of the Union Army, smart in their new dark blue uniforms, began to march out. First two, then four, then six, until a continual column of recruits led from the sidrat to the open double doors of the barn and beyond, all singing *John Brown's Body*, the marching song of the Northern soldiers.

'But that is impossible,' Lady Jennifer whispered. 'All those men were inside that box?'

'Shhh!' The Doctor put his finger to his lips. 'I'm counting.'

At least a hundred soldiers marched from the sidrat. No one spoke again until their singing had receded into the distance.

Zoe said, 'That thing must be bigger inside than outside, just like the TARDIS.'

'I know.' The Doctor approached the sidrat cautiously. 'Jamie, you keep an eye out.'

Zoe joined the Doctor at the sidrat's open door. As they both stepped inside, Jamie called, 'Zoe—Doctor, be careful!'

'This is some terrible trick,' said Lady Jennifer. 'That thing appeared from nowhere.'

'It takes a bit of understanding,' Jamie admitted. He tensed. 'What's that coming?'

Somewhere beyond the barn shots were fired. Jamie rushed to the gaping door of the sidrat, calling inside. 'Doctor! Someone's coming, I think.'

The door closed by itself. The barn was once more filled with the strange sound as the sidrat dematerialised before Jamie's eyes.

The Doctor and Zoe were in a long gloomily-lit corridor. Pale globes of light set in the wall stretched as far as Zoe could see.

'Doctor, it *is* like the TARDIS—bigger inside than out. Who else has space-time machines like yours?'

The Doctor looked uneasy. 'There is an explanation, but I hope ...' He stopped.

'What is it, Doctor?'

He had turned and was hurrying back down the corridor to the corner they had just rounded. Zoe followed, in time to look over his shoulder as the door closed. All at once she felt the floor shuddering.

'We've taken off!' she yelled.

'Perhaps this will take us where we want to go,' the Doctor answered calmly.

'Where *you* want to go.' The floor had stopped shuddering now. She guessed the sidrat had dematerialised and was now moving through space, time or both.

'What's down here?' The Doctor had found another long corridor. Set in the wall at regular intervals were circular viewing windows. He looked in the first one. 'Indeed, very much what I expected, Zoe.'

She looked. In a large partly-lit room stood a line of German soldiers. They stood to attention, eyes open and looking straight ahead. 'They've all been hypnotised,' she said.

The Doctor had already moved to the next circular window. Zoe raced after him. In an identical room was a column of Roman legionaries, also standing to attention like toy soldiers in a box, eyes glazed.

'What are they all here for?'

'They're going to fight, Zoe. That's what soldiers are for.'

The floor started to shudder again. 'Do you think we're materialising again, Doctor?'

59

'Yes, Zoe. Perhaps now we shall get the answers to some of our questions ...'

Jamie and Lady Jennifer hid behind the bales of straw.

'Your friends,' Lady Jennifer whispered, 'what's happened to them?'

'I don't know,' Jamie answered, frightened at being on his own now. 'Don't expect me to explain these things ...'

She put her fingers to her lips. The people they had heard were closer now. A group of weary Confederate soldiers staggered into the barn, glad of somewhere to rest. Two were freshly wounded; blood spattered their light grey uniforms.

'Where did all them Yankee *ree*-cruits come from?' said one man, flopping down on the straw. 'I'm darned sure I picked off two of them.' He patted his rifle affectionately.

Lady Jennifer could not take her eyes off one of the wounded men. He had lain down in pain and tiredness and no one was taking any notice of him.

'I've got to help that young man,' she whispered to Jamie.

'Don't be daft,' he whispered back. 'They'll say we're spies or something ...'·

But she did not listen. To Jamie's amazement she stood up for everyone to see. 'I must help the wounded,' she announced, moving around the straw bale to get to the young man. She had all the self-confidence of her class background; it did not cross her mind that the soldiers would harm her.

For a second the soldiers were too surprised to move. Then the man who had just killed two Yankees raised his rifle.

'You stop right where you are, ma'am.' He got to his feet and, instinctively, checked the back of the bale that Lady Jennifer had just appeared from. 'I'll be durned,' he laughed. 'There's a man here wearing a

60

skirt!' He levelled the rifle at Jamie. 'You come out, boy!'

Jamie emerged. 'It's a kilt,' he said. 'I'm from Scotland.'

Another soldier had got to his feet. 'I'm Corporal Leroy Thompson of the 3rd Georgia Battalion,' he said, introducing himself. 'What are you folks doing here?'

Lady Jennifer was already applying a make-do tourniquet to the wounded soldier. 'We are travellers,' she said coolly. 'I come from England.'

Corporal Thompson looked impressed. 'I reckon you do by that strange accent you got. England's on the side of the South, ain't it?'

'I believe the British Government did favour your cause,' she said, still busy trying to help the soldier. 'Not about slavery but about independence. This man needs water.'

A soldier stepped forward with a metal bottle. 'You a nurse or something?'

'Something,' she said, taking the water bottle.

'We have a little food,' one of the men said, opening his knapsack. 'You folks care to join us?'

'That's very good of you,' Jamie said.

'It ain't much,' the man apologised. 'But I guess we all got to help each other——'

A Southern officer stepped into the doorway of the barn. He wore a wide-brimmed hat and a long grey topcoat with a smart belt. Where he stood a shadow fell across his face. Corporal Leroy Thompson stood to attention.

'Who are these people?' asked the officer.

'Travellers,' said Corporal Thompson. 'The lady's from England and the boy's from . . .'

'Scotland,' said Jamie, realising Thompson had probably never heard of his home country before today.

'That's right,' said the corporal. 'That's why he wears a skirt.' He grinned.

'I think you are mistaken,' said the officer, his voice

cold. 'These are Northern spies, enemies of the South.'

'But, sir,' the corporal started to say.

'Enemies of our cause, corporal. The man is a Yankee soldier dressed in women's clothes. The woman is a spy ...'

All the soldiers were getting to their feet now. In an unnatural voice Corporal Thompson said, 'The man is a Yankee, the woman a spy ...'

'What do we do with Yankees?' the officer asked.

The wounded man Lady Jennifer had helped struggled to sit up. 'We kill them, sir, we kill them!'

'First we shall take them prisoner,' said the officer. 'Tie them up!'

As the soldiers surrounded Lady Jennifer and Jamie the officer stepped from the shadow. Light fell across his face. It was Major von Weich, last seen in the 1917 German trench.

6

The Process

After the floor stopped shuddering a full minute elapsed before the sidrat's door opened. The Doctor and Zoe waited, their backs pressed against the wall of a little alcove, the only cover they could find in case someone came in. Indeed, the moment the door opened two men in black overalls entered.

'This one is playing tricks again,' said the first man, referring to a notebook. 'Control says it made delivery to America 1862, but failed to deliver to the German side in the 1917 Zone and to the Roman war.' He looked up. 'Now the Chinese sector wants more specimens to fight the Japanese in 1936.'

'They'll have to wait,' said his companion. 'We never have enough time to do a proper service. If I had my way ...'

They went down a corridor, the man complaining about the pressures of his job. The Doctor and Zoe crept from their hiding place. Beyond the open door was a brilliantly lit metal floor and a steel wall.

"Not much of a view,' said Zoe.

'But I think we have found the blank centre of the map,' said the Doctor. 'Come on.'

They stepped out. Their sidart was one of four similar tall black boxes standing in a large metal chamber. Metal corridors led off at either end of the chamber. An officer of the 19th century Austro-Hungarian army came along, chatting with a man in civilian clothes of the same period. Neither took any notice of the Doctor and Zoe.

'Let's follow,' the Doctor whispered.

As they trailed the Austro-Hungarian officer they passed another man in a black overall who sat at a console at the end of the line of sidrats.

'He, I imagine,' the Doctor whispered, 'controls these things.'

They passed through several corridors, glanced into study rooms and libraries and kept seeing men dressed as officers from the armies of world history. They even saw two young women dressed in blue slacks and shirts with scarlet neckerchiefs and blue berets.

'The Spanish Civil War,' the Doctor said quietly. 'Women fought in the front line there.'

Zoe noted that most of the people they came across were going in the same direction as the couple they were following. Soon the reason became obvious. The Austro-Hungarian officer arrived at double steel doors, both wide open. Either side stood guards in silver metallic uniforms carrying stun-guns.

'The lecture has already started,' said one of the guards. 'Take your places quietly.'

Through the double doors they found themselves in a huge room—the war room. At one end a wiry man with a small white beard was addressing a mixed group of Romans, Germans, Aztec warriors, soldiers from all ages. The Doctor and Zoe quietly sat down at the back.

'Since you are newly arrived from the home planet,' the scientist with the white beard was saying, 'you may not be aware of our main problem. It is to keep the specimen's personality as a fighting man, while at the same time placing him under our control. As you know, we take human specimens from their own world and, after the process, put them into a sector of this planet that we have made to look the same.'

'So this isn't Earth!' Zoe whispered.

'Shhh,' said the Doctor. 'I had rather guessed that.'

'With most human specimens,' the scientist went on, 'the process is lasting. But with certain humans of strong character the effect of the process fades.'

A man dressed as a Roundhead from the days of Oliver Cromwell put up his hand. 'How often does this happen?'

'Our failure rate is only five per cent, or one in twenty,' replied the scientist. 'It is not much, but these individuals cause us a lot of trouble. They find they can pass through the time zone barriers, and some have joined together into resistance groups. They are upsetting our master plan.' He paused to let the importance of his words sink in. 'To overcome this problem I have further refined our processing techniques. To demonstrate my new process I have chosen a particularly difficult specimen. This man shook off the process completely.' The scientist turned to one of the guards in silver metallic uniform. 'Bring in the specimen.'

The guard turned and opened a small door. Another guard came through the open door pushing a wheel chair. Strapped to the chair was a young British army officer—Lieutenant Carstairs.

Zoe grabbed the Doctor's arm in excitement. 'He's all right! They didn't kill him!'

The scientist looked down at the helpless Carstairs. 'Describe what you can see.'

Carstairs looked around. 'A room filled with a lot of scientific mumbo-jumbo. Strange people in funny clothes.'

'As you see,' the scientist said to the assembled group, 'he is conscious of his surroundings and hostile. Now watch.'

The scientist fitted a metal cowl over Carstairs's head. Carstairs struggled violently against the bonds holding his wrists and ankles, but to no avail. The scientist went to a little control panel and activated some switches. The metal cowl gave a low humming sound.

'Can't we help him?' Zoe whispered.

'Not now,' the Doctor whispered back. 'Perhaps later.'

'This machine,' the scientist explained, 'is only a prototype. Soon we shall have machines that can process large groups of specimens all at the same time.' He checked his dials. 'That should be enough. Release the specimen.'

While the guards unstrapped Carstairs, the scientist removed the cowl. Carstairs was sitting in the wheelchair quite relaxed now.

'What is your name?' asked the scientist.

'Jeremy Carstairs.'

'I am your superior officer,' the scientist snapped. Instantly Carstairs got out of the chair and jumped to attention. 'Sorry, sir.'

'Where are you, Carstairs?'

Now Carstairs looked confused. 'Well, sir, I'm ...'

'You are in my office at headquarters,' the scientist told him.

'That's right, sir. I am in your office at headquarters.'

'Very good,' said the scientist. He pointed to the cowl and the control panel. 'What are those things?'

Carstairs looked. 'Sir?'

'You can't see anything where I am pointing?'

'No, sir. Sorry, sir.'

'Excellent.' The scientist turned back to the group. 'Objects beyond his comprehension are now invisible to him.' He turned back to Carstairs. 'Who are all these people?'

Carstairs considered. 'My brother officers, sir.' Looking around the group his eyes fell on Zoe and the Doctor. He raised an accusing finger. 'Except those two, sir! They are German spies!'

'He's playing a game,' said Zoe, not yet concerned.

'I don't think so,' said the Doctor. 'Sit tight and hope for the best.'

'German spies?' said the scientist. 'Whatever gives you that idea? These are all your masters.' He turned with a smile to the group. 'When I said the word "masters" just then he heard the words "brother officers"!'

'I implore you to believe me, sir. Those two are spies. While thousands of British heroes are giving their lives for King and Country, those two are collecting information ...'

'Take him away!' the scientist snapped at the guards. Carstairs was hurried back through the little door, still protesting. 'As I said,' the scientist continued to the group, 'I chose a particularly difficult specimen. Perhaps we should try another.' The scientist was about to call for another specimen, but to his surprise one of the listeners was speaking up.

'It should have been possible to re-process that man, don't you think?' The Doctor had risen from his place and was moving through the group towards the processing machine. 'Let me look at this thing.'

The scientist was outraged. 'Kindly return to your place!'

'Personally,' said the Doctor, closing in on the scientist and his equipment, 'I think the man was unbalanced. Fancy calling any of us spies.' The Doctor started to examine the cowl and the control panel.

The scientist became defensive. 'He was probably tracking down German spies before he came here. It's some fixation with him. Please leave the equipment alone!'

'I would,' said the Doctor, removing an inspection cap and peering inside, 'except that it is defective. This circuit here is overloading the neural paths. Did you de-process that man completely before you gave this demonstration?'

'It is none of your business! Please return to your seat!'

The Doctor looked at him. 'It is very much my business. How can we carry out our great plan if any equipment isn't working properly? Now, I asked you a simple question: was that man de-processed before the experiment?'

'There was no need,' the scientist answered uneasily. 'His processing had already lapsed. You saw that for yourself.'

'What I saw,' said the Doctor, 'was a specimen whose processing had *partly* lapsed. He should have been completely de-processed before you started again. Still, I don't suppose you can do that on this machine ...'

'Of course we can,' said the scientist, proudly. 'It's simply a matter of re-arranging the circuits. Let me show you.' He disconnected a number of wires and reconnected them with different terminals. 'There you are. This machine can now remove all traces of any previous processing.'

'That's fascinating,' said the Doctor. 'I must congratulate you. I hope our little chat will be useful for both of us. I will now return to my place.'

With a smile the Doctor made his way back through the group to Zoe. As he refound his place a loud *ping* sounded from wall loudspeakers. Everyone present became alert.

'What is it?' Zoe asked.

Before the Doctor could answer, the double doors had been opened. The War Chief stepped in, guards on either side.

'Was the experiment successful?' he asked the scientist.

'Partially, sir.'

'Only partially?' The War Chief walked up to the processing machine.

'I think we have found the cause, sir.' The scientist treated the War Chief with great respect and was clearly frightened of him. 'As a matter of fact, one of the students has been of great help to me. Perhaps he should be transferred to the scientific team.'

'Really? And which one was that?' The War Chief ran his eyes over the group.

The scientist pointed. 'Over there, sir.'

The War Chief's eyes came to rest on the Doctor. Zoe thought she detected a moment of mutual recognition between the Doctor and the War Chief, as though they had once known each other.

'Zoe,' the Doctor breathed urgently. 'Run—and don't stop!'

Obediently Zoe got up, turned and ran, the Doctor behind her.

The War Chief called to his guards, 'Fire!'

The *zing* of stun-guns rang out. A Samurai knight of ancient Japan was accidentally hit and crashed to the floor. The Doctor jumped over him. As Zoe reached the double doors she paused, looking to the Doctor to be told which way.

The Doctor called, 'Just keep going!'

Outside in the corridor a queue of officers from all times in history was waiting to go in for the next

The scientist looked up from his processing machine. 'What are you doing here? There's a security alarm out for you.' His hand moved towards an emergency button.

'Not me,' said the Doctor. 'They were after that girl. I tried to catch her but the guards got her first. Has she been killed yet?' He tried to sound casual.

The scientist shook his head. 'She's with Security being questioned.'

'I see,' said the Doctor, pretending not to be very interested. 'And what about this fellow? I would think it a great privilege if I can stand and watch what you're doing. In fact, what exactly *are* you doing?'

'What you suggested. I shall completely de-process him first before the re-processing.' The scientist, busy making adjustments to the machine's circuits, glanced at Carstairs. 'You might help by fixing those clamps to his wrists and ankles.'

'Indeed I shall. Once completely back to normal, he's likely to be dangerous, isn't he?' The Doctor gave a good impression of binding Carstairs to the chair. 'There, that should hold him in.'

The scientist switched on the machine. As it hummed pleasantly Carstairs relaxed from his rigid, upright way of sitting. After only a few moments the scientist switched off. 'He should now be completely de-processed.'

Carstairs shook his head, confused. 'Where ... where am I?' He looked up. 'Doctor!'

'He's not your doctor,' the scientist said, scornfully. 'I wonder if this de-processing has really worked.' The scientist turned to inspect the machine.

'I think it has,' said the Doctor. 'Lieutenant Carstairs is now free in mind and body.'

Carstairs was out of the chair before the scientist realised what had happened. He grabbed the scientist's arms. 'What do we do with him, Doctor?'

'Into the chair, quick.'

Carstairs pushed the scientist into the chair and held him while the Doctor attached the clamps to his wrists and ankles. 'And now, sir, you are going to tell

73

me where my young friend is being questioned.'

'I shall tell you nothing!'

The Doctor brought the cowl down over the scientist's head. 'You are in your normal mental state. What if I turned on this machine now that it is set to de-processing?'

The scientist cowered back in the chair. 'I ... I shall become an idiot. But you wouldn't! You couldn't!'

'I don't wish to destroy an intelligence,' said the Doctor, 'even yours. But my friend's safety comes first. You have two seconds to save your own mind.' His fingers touched the 'on' control.

'Turn left,' said the scientist. 'Second corridor on the left. You'll find a black door.'

The Doctor reached into his pockets and brought out bandages with which he gagged the scientist. He put out the lights in the room so that anyone looking through the window in the door would not see what had happened. Then he opened the door and stepped into the corridor, followed by Carstairs.

'Let us stroll gently,' the Doctor suggested. 'We don't want to draw attention to ourselves.'

During their gentle stroll the Doctor explained everything he knew to Carstairs. Carstairs's memory was still vague as to how and when he was abducted from his own world and brought to this one, but he could remember everything from the time he met the Doctor.

'A black door,' said the Doctor, pointing. 'Our friend told the truth.'

'How shall we rescue Zoe?' Carstairs asked.

'I have no idea,' the Doctor answered honestly. 'But let's start by opening this door.'

He yanked open the black door and stepped inside. A guard whirled around, levelling a stun-gun. Zoe was slumped in a chair.

'Get out of here,' the guard shouted.

The Doctor ignored him. He walked straight across the room to Zoe. 'My dear, what have they done to you?'

74

The guard turned around to keep his stun-gun trained on the Doctor. 'I think you're the man we're looking for . . .'

His words ended there. Carstairs had stepped in behind him. He brought the butt of his service revolver sharply across the back of the guard's neck, just below his helmet. The guard fell.

'They questioned me,' Zoe moaned, head in hands. 'They used that.' She pointed to a pair of giant earphones. 'I saw pictures of . . . of the resistance. They think I'm a member. They wanted me to identify people . . .'

While Zoe talked the Doctor tried on the earphones. He activated the little machine to which they were connected and instantly began to see mental images of faces—a soldier in Turkish uniform, a British Boer War sergeant from 1899, a British private of 1917. He switched off.

'Fascinating little gadget,' he said. 'So at least we know there is a resistance organisation.'

'How can there be,' said Carstairs, 'if all the soldiers are under the thumb of these bounders?'

'The effect of the process sometimes wears off, as it did with you and Lady Jennifer.' The Doctor turned back to Zoe. 'Can you remember all the faces you saw?'

'Of course,' she said confidently.

'Then we must return to the time zones and organise these people into one huge resistance army.'

'And how,' said Carstairs, 'do we get back there?'

'Same way as we came,' said the Doctor. 'Follow me. We've played hide and seek so far. Let's hope our luck holds.'

'You will all be recaptured now,' von Weich said calmly. Jamie admired the man's nerve. 'Something is about to happen beyond your understanding. Before you can regain your wits, you will be our prisoners. Then we shall deal with your minds and you will forget everything.'

75

Some of the resistance fighters were still so impressed by the telecommunications unit that they looked inclined to believe him.

'It's like a picture in a frame,' said the Negro. 'Only it ain't no picture.'

'A device invented long after your time,' said von Weich. 'Any moment now you will be even more puzzled.'

Jamie said, 'You expect one of your transports to come and save you?'

Von Weich nodded. 'That's right. You will be overwhelmed.'

'Why are you doing this?' Lady Jennifer asked. 'Who are you and where do you come from?'

'That would take a lot of explaining,' von Weich replied. 'Most of it would be impossible for you to understand.'

She bridled. 'Because I'm a woman?'

'No,' he said. 'Because you are a human——'

The sound of a materialising sidrat filled the barn.

'What's that?' said Sergeant Russell. Already the sound was increasing in intensity.

'Quick,' said Jamie, 'everyone hide! A box is going to appear right there,' he said, pointing to the centre of the barn. 'Someone'll come out of it. We've got to grab them. First grab him!' He pointed at von Weich.

The sound was striking terror into the soldiers, all except Sergeant Russell. He alone acted on Jamie's advice and grabbed von Weich.

'All right, I've got him!'

Jamie joined the sergeant in throwing von Weich to the ground in the stall. Together they sat on him and hid themselves and the struggling von Weich behind a mound of straw.

'What now?' asked the sergeant.

Jamie kept his eyes on the centre of the barn. 'You watch.'

The sound was deafening now. Everyone had hidden, not so much as a tactic but through sheer terror. Quite suddenly the sidrat materialised in exactly the same spot as before. Once it was totally visible, the sound ceased. The American Negro soldier raised his head on the other side of the barn.

'Glory be! It ain't possible!'

Jamie waved to him to keep down. 'Shut up.'

They waited. Below Jamie, von Weich lay quite still. A full half minute passed before the sidrat's door opened. Two guards in silvery uniforms stepped out carrying stun-guns. They looked around but saw no one. One of them noticed the revealed telecommunications unit and walked over to it. Silently, Sergeant Russell drew his revolver.

The Negro looked up again, holding his old-fashioned rifle. 'Halt! You're our prisoners now——'

The guard at the door of the sidrat wheeled round and fired his stun gun. The Negro fell. At the same moment Sergeant Russell fired his revolver up through the straw at the guard approaching the video screen. The guard stumbled backwards, dead before he hit the ground. The Frenchman raised his head for a moment to draw the other guard's fire. As the stun-gun *zinged*, the German private shot the guard dead. Everyone looked up from their hiding places.

'Be careful,' Jamie warned. 'There could be hundreds of them in there.'

The soldiers took no heed. To them the sidrat looked only large enough to carry two people—and both lay dead on the barn floor. Cautiously they moved forward to inspect the mysterious black box.

'*Le noir,*' said the French soldier, looking at the Negro's body, '' 'e is dead but no mark.'

Sergeant Russell picked up one of the stun-guns. 'A gun without bullets,' he said, finding no hole at the end of the snout.

'This thing,' said Jamie, indicating the sidrat, 'we've got to get into it before the door closes. It'll take us to the place where all the trouble starts from.'

'I quite agree,' said Lady Jennifer. 'We must take the battle into the enemy's camp.' She stood by the open door, ready to step into the sidrat.

The sergeant smiled. 'I admire your courage, ma'am, but ladies don't fight.'

77

'Why not? I believe in votes for women, so why shouldn't we fight if necessary?'

'Because,' he said, trying to think of a reason, 'because you're a nurse. In our camp we have plenty of wounded men. You're more use to them alive than dead.'

'I don't know the way to your camp,' she protested.

He pointed to the Chinese soldier. 'He'll take you.' He looked at her appealingly. 'Some of our boys are badly hurt, ma'am. They need you.'

'Yes, but . . .'

'He's right,' said Jamie. 'England will be proud of you, Lady Jennifer.' Inwardly he bit his lip. As a 1745 Highlander his enemy was England.

'All right,' she agreed. 'I hope we meet again, Jamie.'

'Vot about him?' The German soldier aimed his rifle at von Weich.

'He comes with us,' said Jamie. 'He could be useful making this thing work.'

'On your feet,' the sergeant shouted at von Weich. 'Over here.'

Von Weich obeyed the command submissively.

'He's being too good to be true,' Jamie warned. 'We'll have to watch him. Let's get into this thing before the door closes.'

He led the way, followed by the Frenchman and the German and the two British soldiers from the Boer War. The door closed the moment they were inside and the barn filled with the sound of the sidrat dematerialising.

The Doctor's luck had held very well. With Zoe and Lieutenant Carstairs he had retraced his steps to the sidrat bay. No sidrats were present when the trio arrived.

'What is this place?' Carstairs asked.

'Machines like the TARDIS arrive here,' Zoe explained.

'Oh yes,' he said. 'I see.' He did not understand at all. But now his mind was overflowing with technical

78

innovations that were beyond him.

'We should wait here,' said the Doctor. 'One of these boxes will materialise and we shall all get into it. Then we can get back to the time zones.' He had found a suitable vantage point where they were not too obvious but could see the bay.

A loud *ping* rang through the metal corridors.

Carstairs said, 'They've found the man we tied up.'

'Or the guard you knocked out,' added Zoe.

A troop of silver-uniformed guards came running down a corridor, carrying stun-guns. Carstairs reached for his revolver.

'Wait,' said the Doctor. The guards had seen them but kept running. 'They're not for us, I think.'

The guards stopped within hearing. A senior guard addressed the others. 'A sidrat's coming in. It hasn't given the correct signal. Pirates may be aboard. Take up positions.'

While the Doctor watched helplessly, the guards ran to positions of hiding.

'Pirates?' said Zoe. 'But how?'

'I don't know, Zoe,' said the Doctor. 'I only hope ...'

His words were drowned by the materialisation sound. A black box appeared in the bay and the sound stopped.

'By jingo,' said Carstairs. 'That's jolly clever.'

'Shhh,' said the Doctor.

The sidrat's door opened. Jamie stepped out, immediately followed by the resistance fighters and von Weich. Zoe was about to cry out a warning but the Doctor put his hand over her mouth.

'Which way?' asked Sergeant Russell.

'I don't know,' said Jamie. 'Maybe it doesn't matter——'

All the guards fired at once.

'Not me!' von Weich screamed. 'I'm one of you——'

He reeled over as a stun-gun hit him.

The Doctor, Zoe and Carstairs watched silently as the guards emerged from their hiding places and came forward to drag away the lifeless bodies.

7

The Security Chief

The scientist approached the black door nervously. No one relished being summoned by the Security Chief. His fears increased as he went inside and saw the Chief's stormy expression.

'Sit down,' said the Security Chief.

The scientist sat. Two of the Chief's guards were tending a guard lying on the floor.

'Is his neck broken?' asked the Chief.

'No, sir,' said one of the guards. 'Bruised but not broken.'

'Then remove him.'

They dragged the guard out.

The Security Chief stood behind his desk. He was a small man who enjoyed immense power; he did not like people to see how short he was, so often he remained standing. Different from the War Chief, the Security Chief wore a simple black uniform without braid or piping. It made him look very sinister.

'I understand you were overpowered and tied up?' he said.

'Yes,' replied the scientist.

'I believe some of the resistance group who infiltrated this base arrived on the planet without being brought here by us.'

'Impossible!'

'Is it? The girl I questioned spoke of a space-time machine. The man who tricked you understood our mental processing equipment. Wasn't that odd?'

'I suppose so,' said the scientist, who hadn't really thought about it. 'But time and space travel—who else in the entire galaxy knows about that?'

'The people whose knowledge we are using,' said

the Security Chief. 'Remember how we obtained that knowledge...'

'Through the War Chief.'

'Exactly! He is a traitor to his own people, the Time Lords.' The Security Chief looked at the scientist, awaiting a response.

'Are you ... are you suggesting he's bringing in his own people?'

'He joined us because he wanted power. Perhaps there are others of his people who have the same ambition. For instance, this person the girl spoke of as the Doctor.'

'Can you prove any of this?'

'I am simply giving an opinion,' the Security Chief said honestly.

'I wish you wouldn't give your opinions to me,' said the scientist. 'If you have these ideas you should tell the War Lord on the home planet.'

'When I have proof.' The Security Chief placed a hand on the scientist's shoulder. 'You can help me. Before you re-process those stupid soldiers whom we ambushed and stunned, study them carefully. If you find any of them who have never been processed, send them to me for questioning. And don't mention it to the War Chief.'

The scientist's throat had gone dry. 'But I ... I don't want to get mixed up in intrigue. The War Chief has total authority here.'

'And I,' said the Security Chief, 'have power of life and death. You are my friend, are you not? As friends we should work together.'

The Security Chief squeezed the scientist's shoulder and gave a smile that sent shivers down the scientist's spine.

Lieutenant Carstairs looked along the rows of different coloured jackets hanging on racks.

'A uniform for all occasions, what?'

'We're in the wardrobe,' said the Doctor, delighted.

He held out the sleeve of a jacket with a row of tiny buttons. 'I'd say that's the Russian Army of the 18th Century. Catherine the Great had the buttons put on to stop her soldiers from wiping their noses on their sleeves.'

Zoe called from across the vast room. 'There are metal suits over here.'

The Doctor looked up. 'Suits of armour, Zoe. Very impractical. If the wearer fell over he was too heavy ever to get up again.'

'Why did you want to come in here?' Carstairs asked.

'This is next to the place where that scientist was going to re-process you.' The Doctor moved over to the wall. 'If we were able to see into there . . .' He got out his sonic screwdriver, made an adjustment and held it to the wall. A small hole appeared.

Carstairs was astonished. 'How did you do that?'

'I disintegrated that part of the wall's molecular structure. Now let us see what we can see.' The Doctor peered through the hole.

The resistance fighters stun-gunned in the ambush lay on the floor. Two silver-uniformed guards were lifting the young French soldier onto an inspection table. The scientist put a headset on the man, touched a button and watched a little screen.

'Put him in the re-processing chair,' he ordered.

The guards sat the Frenchman in the chair that Carstairs had once occupied, clamping his wrists and ankles.

'The one in the skirt,' said the scientist. 'Put him on the table.'

The Doctor turned to Zoe and Carstairs. 'I can see Jamie,' he said excitedly. 'He's unconscious but he's alive.'

Carstairs was puzzled. 'The guns didn't kill?'

'Apparently not. They were adjusted to stun.' The Doctor returned his attention to the hole. 'Now let' see . . .'

The headset was on Jamie. The scientist was looking at the little screen, puzzled.

'Something wrong?' asked a guard.

'Yes,' said the scientist. 'Very wrong. Take this specimen to the Security Chief. Tell him that this skirted man was never processed in the first place.'

'How is that possible?' said the guard.

'Have your Chief explain. He has an opinion.'

The two guards lifted up Jamie to carry him out. As they approachd the door, it opened. The War Chief stepped into the processing room with his two personal bodyguards. The scientist paled at the sight of him.

'Have you commenced re-processing yet?' asked the War Chief, pleasantly.

'Er, I was just going to start with this one.' The scientist indicated the Frenchman strapped in the chair.

'And this one? Where is he going?' The War Chief looked at the two guards carrying out Jamie.

'The Security Chief,' mumbled the scientist. 'He wanted to question one of them before re-processing.'

'Why did you select that one?'

'He . . . His brain patterns are different, sir.'

'How different?'

Through the hole the Doctor could clearly see the scientist's Adam's apple working up and down in his throat. 'How is he different, sir?'

'At least you are not deaf,' said the War Chief. 'Yes, I clearly asked how are his brain patterns different.'

The scientist's mouth opened but no speech came out.

'Come now,' said the War Chief in a friendly way. 'We have no secrets, do we?'

'He . . . I mean, I think . . . Well, it's possible that he hasn't been processed before.'

For a moment the War Chief said nothing. Then he smiled. 'How extraordinary. Well, I suggest you keep me informed of any such . . . unusual developments.' He turned to go and paused in the doorway. 'We are very proud of your work, you know. The War Lord remarked only yesterday that without your genius none of this would have been possible.'

The scientist glowed with delight. 'Oh, thank you.'

'Thank *you*,' said the War Chief and left the processing room with his two bodyguards.

Alone, the scientist turned to the unconscious Frenchman strapped in the chair. 'Did you hear that? The War Lord says I'm a genius!'

The Doctor turned to Carstairs. 'We've got to get in there before the guards come back.' He studied the wall. 'If I could change its entire molecular structure...'

'There is another way,' said Carstairs. 'It's only a dividing panel. Watch.' He put his hand into the hole and quietly lifted out the entire panel. 'You were saying something about its molecular structure, sir?' He put the panel down to one side.

As Zoe stifled a laugh, the Doctor and Carstairs stepped into the processing room. Carstairs had his revolver drawn. The scientist, about to work on the young Frenchman, had his back turned.

'May I, sir,' said the Doctor, 'add my praise to that of the War Lord? You truly are a genius.'

The scientist half turned. 'Thank you. Thank you very much.'

'And may I,' said Lieutenant Carstairs, 'request you to raise your hands?'

The scientist swung round. 'Oh, dear ...'

Jamie became conscious to find himself strapped to a chair. The Security Chief was lifting a metal cowl from his head.

'Feeling all right now?' asked the Security Chief.

'Yes, fine.' Jamie tried to move; it was then he realised he was bound to the chair. 'Hey, what's this?'

'I am going to question you.' The Security Chief snapped his fingers and a guard brought forward another metal cowl. 'I have just un-stunned you. Now I am going to cause you intense pain.' He paused. 'Unless you answer my questions truthfully.'

Jamie looked at the cowl they were about to place over his head. 'Let me hear the questions first.'

'How did you arrive on this planet?'

'In a thing called the TARDIS. It flies through time and space. Will you undo me now?'

The Security Chief gave his spine-chilling smile. 'You like making jokes, do you?'

'We Scots are very humorous.'

The Security Chief regarded his prisoner. His hand rested lightly on the cowl, one finger tapping its metal surface. 'Who is the Doctor?'

Jamie didn't answer.

'Fix the cowl,' said the Security Chief.

The guard moved forward to put the cowl directly over Jamie's head.

'I don't know who he is,' Jamie said quickly. 'He almost told me, but then he didn't. It's no good hurting me with that thing. I can't tell you anything else.'

'Do you know, I think I believe you. Tell me, what sort of man is this Doctor?'

'He's a good man,' Jamie said.

The Security Chief spoke his thoughts as he created a picture in his own mind. 'A good man of mysterious origins who travels through time and space ...' He returned his attention to Jamie. 'I want to show you to someone else.' He moved to the door. 'You won't go away, will you?'

'I'll sit right here,' said Jamie, unable to move.

'Good,' said the Security Chief. 'I like a specimen with a sense of fun.' Quietly he left the security room.

Jamie looked at the guard. 'Any chance you could unstrap one hand? I want to scratch my nose.'

The guard did not reply.

'Just one hand,' said Jamie. 'I can't do you any harm with only one hand.'

Instead of helping Jamie, the guard seemed intrigued by the pain helmet and the machine to which it was attached. His fingers played across the controls.

'You be careful,' said Jamie. 'Remember I'm under this thing ...'

The guard's finger hit the 'on' button. Instantly Jamie had a mild headache.

'Hey, turn that thing off!'

The guard looked at Jamie's pained expression and

grinned. He searched for the control that would increase the pain—and found it. He edged the pointer round two calibrations.

Jamie closed his eyes in sudden agony. His brain was filled with stabbing pains and blinding explosions. 'Please,' he moaned, 'I told the truth . . . You shouldn't do that . . . Please . . . Help me . . .'

The pain ceased as suddenly as it had begun. Hands were at Jamie's wrists and ankles, releasing him. He opened his eyes to see the room filled with drab khaki uniforms, similar to those he had seen on the 1917 British Front Line.

'It's all right, Jamie,' the Doctor was saying. 'It's me.' The Doctor stood before him dressed in a voluminous general's greatcoat.

Jamie tried to get the others into focus. 'Lady Jennifer,' he said, still confused.

'It's me,' said Zoe. 'They've got every type of uniform here. Do you think it suits me?' She looked down at her khaki tunic and the long skirt of a Volunteer Ambulance Driver of the First World War.

The two Boer War soldiers, also dressed in British army uniform of eighteen years later than their time in history, were tying up the guard who had tortured Jamie. 'Perhaps we should leave him under that gadget,' said the private. 'And turn on the juice!'

'I think we'd do better,' suggested Lieutenant Carstairs, 'to get out of here as quickly as possible.'

'Get this stuff on, Jamie.' The Doctor produced from under his greatcoat a khaki cap and another greatcoat. 'And put this over your face.' He held out a mask with two circular glass windows to see through and a snout.

'What is it?'

'A gas mask.' The Doctor called to the others in the room, 'Quickly! Gas masks back on—and off we go!'

The Boer War sergeant's muffled voice boomed through his gas mask as they marched down the corridor.

'Left, right, left, right, left, right . . .'

The group made a fine spectacle as the Doctor led them through one corridor after another towards the sidrat materialisation bay. Officers of many armies jumped out of their way and some even saluted.

'Left, right, left, right,' the sergeant continued to shout. In an undertone he said to the Doctor, 'Do you really know the way?'

'Of course I do,' said the Doctor, hoping he could remember. To his delight as they turned yet another corner the sidrat bay appeared before them. Not a sidrat was to be seen.

'This is it,' he said.

'Left, right, left, right. Compan-ee-ee, halt!'

They all stopped. The black-overalled technician at the control console half turned.

'Where to?' he asked.

'1917,' said the Doctor. 'British sector.'

The technician looked at his check list. 'Nothing about that here.'

'The reason you have not been informed,' said the Doctor, 'is that our journey is unofficial.'

'Eh?' The technician was genuinely bewildered.

'Take him,' the Doctor snapped.

Three of the soldiers grabbed the startled man, bound and gagged him, and bundled him out of sight behind the console. Meanwhile the Doctor tugged off his gas mask and sat down to study the controls.

'Now let me see ... First we need to materialise a sidrat.' The Doctor adjusted controls on the console. Instantly the chamber was filled with the strangely familiar materialisation sound.

The Boer War private watched as a sidrat took shape before his eyes. 'I still don't believe that's possible.'

'Now,' said the Doctor, 'I must pre-set its journey for 1917 and off we go.' He made further adjustments to the controls.

Zoe eyed him curiously. 'Doctor, how do you know what to do with those controls? You've never touched them before.'

'I was wondering that,' said Jamie. 'You seem to

know a lot about this place.'

'Just a matter of logic.' The Doctor touched another control. The sidrat's door opened. 'Everybody get in, and no more questions.'

They all rushed into the safety of the sidrat, the Doctor carrying a knapsack.

'What have you got in there, Doctor?' Jamie asked.

'The solution to the problem,' replied the Doctor. 'All of you, prepare for take off!'

The door of the sidrat closed and the floor shuddered as they started their journey.

The Security Chief was walking along the corridor to his own security room accompanied by the War Chief. He was trying to make the War Chief hurry, but, in theory at least, the War Chief was his superior.

'I really cannot understand why you wish me to see a prisoner,' said the War Chief.

'He has never been processed.'

'Oh, you mean the young man who wears a skirt? Our scientist showed him to me.'

'He did?' This was news to the Security Chief. 'I have questioned him since then. He claims he came here in a space-time machine.'

The War Chief did not reply.

'Isn't that very strange?' said the Security Chief. 'Only your species can travel through space *and* time. You had to teach us how to do it. Isn't that why our War Lord made you the War Chief?'

'What are you trying to say, Security Chief? That you do not trust me?'

Fortunately, the Security Chief did not have to answer this direct question. They had already reached the door to the security room.

'The prisoner is in here,' he said, flinging open the door. 'I shall use the pain process to make him talk——' He found himself looking at his own guard, gagged and strapped in a chair.

The War Chief concealed a smile. 'Another escape? I suggest that before you start doubting me, you might

88

take a little more interest in security. If you will excuse me, I must return to the war room.' He turned and left.

The Security Chief glared at the gagged man. 'You idiot!'

The guard stared back in mute terror. He could read his chief's mind.

'You are strapped in tight,' said the Security Chief. 'The pain cowl is over your head. For what you've done I should turn on the power and leave you!'

The terrain was hilly and wooded. The cart track led between two sharp rises of the land.

'There's nothing to tell us which time zone we're in,' said Lieutenant Carstairs.

Zoe looked at the gentle green scenery. 'You couldn't even tell if there's a war on.'

They had walked at least three miles since leaving the sidrat and now sat in a circle on lush grass by the track. The Doctor shrugged off his general's topcoat, revealing his own clothes beneath.

'It doesn't really matter which zone we're in,' he said. 'The important thing is we have Zoe, and she now knows what all the resistance leaders look like.'

'That's going to be wonderful,' said Sergeant Russell. 'We could never really trust anyone who said they were in the resistance. Now we can all get together and form one big army.'

'Exactly,' said the Doctor. 'The other important thing is that we have this.' He reached into his knapsack and brought out a small silver-coloured box with controls and terminal points.

'What is it?' asked Jamie.

'Before we rescued you we helped ourselves to this from the processing room. It's the head from their machine. With this we can de-process other soldiers.' As he talked the Doctor scrutinised the little box. 'It's a remarkable machine, almost as good as I could have made myself.'

Lieutenant Carstairs stood up. 'Shall we press on?'

'Might as well.' Sergeant Russell started to rise. He stopped half-way. 'Don't look now,' he said, 'but there's someone hiding over there.'

He sank back onto the grass, assuming a lazing position and described exactly where he meant. 'Where this track goes between those two rising bits of land, half-way up on the left—there are some men in those bushes.'

Carstairs made a pretence of rubbing cramp out of his left knee, as though that was the reason he had stood up. Then he too sank back onto the grass, seemingly as unconcerned as a man at a picnic. 'That's an obvious place for an ambush,' he said quietly. 'Do we have to go that way, Doctor?'

'This track must lead somewhere,' said the Doctor. 'You, Jamie and I shall keep to the track. The rest of you could go up that rise of land and come down behind whoever is hiding there.'

'You vill act as decoy?' said the German soldier.

'That's right.' The Doctor got to his feet. 'I suggest we start moving now.'

'But Doctor,' said Zoe, 'why can't we all go up round the top behind them?'

'Because if it is an ambush, my dear, someone has to draw their fire.' The Doctor hoisted over his shoulder the knapsack containing the processing head. 'Now you lot get moving. You must be in position up there to pounce when they make their move.'

He strode off down the track. Carstairs and Jamie scrambled to their feet to follow.

'You heard what he said.' Sergeant Russell got to his feet. 'Off we go, at the double.'

The outflanking party ran towards the rising land, making a wide detour so as not to be seen by whoever was lurking on the little wooded hill. Sergeant Russell acted as pacemaker, urging them on and signalling them to keep very quiet. Soon they were at the top of the rise looking down onto the track. The sergeant pointed downwards into the thicket. Zoe caught glimpses of men in British steel helmets of the 1917 period.

'*Engländer*,' murmured the German.

'*Anglais*,' said the French soldier.

They all held themselves ready to crash down onto the British soldiers at the sergeant's order.

The Doctor, Jamie and Lieutenant Carstairs came into sight, casually walking along the track.

Zoe whispered, 'Perhaps they're resistance fighters like you.'

'We'll soon see,' said the sergeant.

He had no sooner spoken than the chatter of a heavy machine-gun broke out immediately below them. Earth spurted up all around the trio on the track below. Without waiting for the sergeant's command, all the soldiers broke cover and battled their way downhill through the trees and thicket to get at the concealed machine-gun nest. Zoe held back, knowing she could contribute little to the fight taking place on the slope below. She waited to see the Doctor, Jamie and Lieutenant Carstairs rush for cover into the wood on the other side of the track. Then she followed the others down the hill.

The battle had taken less than a minute. Three British machine-gunners lay knocked out by their gun, which was now in the possession of the resistance men.

Sergeant Russell stood up to call to the Doctor. 'It's all right,' he bellowed. 'There are three men here you can de-process with that machine!'

The Doctor, Jamie and Carstairs emerged from hiding on the other side of the track.

'That won't be so easy here,' the Doctor called back. 'But let me take a look at them——'

Suddenly, from all along the wood on the Doctor's side of the track, British soldiers emerged, closing in on the trio.

'The machine-gun,' said the Boer War private urgently. 'Let's turn it on them.'

The sergeant viewed the spectacle below. 'We can't,' he said frowning. 'We'd kill our own friends.'

In silence the little group watched as the three friends were taken prisoner and marched away.

8

Battle for the Château

General Smythe eyed the three prisoners standing before him in his office.

'You have caused a great deal of trouble,' he said. 'But that has now come to an end.' He banged the trestle table at which he was sitting.

'Are we going to have another of your farcical courts martial?' asked the Doctor.

'Not necessary. You have already been condemned to death. As for your two colleagues, they will have a chance to make the supreme sacrifice on a very dangerous section of the front line. They can die for their king and country.'

'You can drop all that nonsense,' said Carstairs. 'This isn't the war. We're not even on our own planet.' He turned to the soldiers guarding them. 'Don't you chaps realise that? This so-called general isn't even a human being.'

The guards looked embarrassed at the prisoner's outburst, but said nothing.

General Smythe smiled. 'They don't understand what you're talking about, Lieutenant. You're wasting your breath.' He turned to the sergeant of the guard. 'Organise a firing squad.'

'Already organised, sir,' said the sergeant.

'How thoughtful of you,' said the general. 'Well, take that one out and shoot him. Be quick about it.'

'Yes, sir!'

The sergeant rattled off orders to two of the guards. They grabbed the Doctor's arms and pinioned them behind his back.

Outraged, Jamie made a grab at one of the soldiers. Another soldier raised his rifle butt and brought it across the back of Jamie's head. Meanwhile, two other

92

soldiers raised their guns menacingly at Lieutenant Carstairs.

'Out with him,' roared General Smythe.

The Doctor was quickly bundled out of the office.

'Keep these two prisoners here,' said the general to the remaining guards. 'I may want a further word with them.'

He rose and went into his bedroom, closing the door.

For some moments Jamie lay where he had fallen. The sergeant of the guard stepped forward, his boots uncomfortably near to Jamie's face.

'You! Up on your feet!'

Jamie felt the back of his head. The rifle butt had raised a lump but there was no blood. Though still dizzy from the blow, he struggled to his feet.

'You're all being made fools of,' he said bitterly. 'The Doctor is the one person who can help you. If you shoot him you're all as good as dead.'

'Prisoner to remain silent!' barked the sergeant.

'It's no good, Jamie,' said Lieutenant Carstairs. 'We walked right into their double ambush. We only have ourselves to blame.'

From the distance they could hear a voice giving commands to the firing squad just outside the château. *'Firing squad, attention! Take positions ... Take aim ... Fire!'*

Jamie closed his eyes. A volley of shots rang out. As his mind dwelt on the death of the Doctor he could hear the shots still ringing in his ears. He could not understand why they continued to fire their rifles and thought it must be his imagination.

'Jamie,' Carstairs was saying, 'listen.'

He opened his eyes. Firing was still continuing, ragged bursts of rifle and now machine-gun fire. The sergeant looked apprehensive.

'Prisoners to lie on the floor, face down.'

The sergeant underlined his command by giving Jamie a shove. Both he and Lieutenant Carstairs lay down.

'Keep them covered,' ordered the sergeant. 'Shoot to kill if necessary.'

While the guards trained their rifles on the two prostrate figures, the sergeant ran to the bedroom door. 'General Smythe, sir! I think we're under attack!'

Outside men were shouting and calling to each other as firing continued. A nearby burst of fire shattered most of the remaining panes of glass in the french windows. All in a moment the french windows burst open. A ragged band of resistance fighters led by Sergeant Russell swarmed in. The guards' guns trained on Jamie and Carstairs were raised to fend off the attackers. Jamie was deafened by the roar of rifles being fired in the enclosed space of the office. A stray bullet hit the ornate chain of the chandelier that kept it attached to the ceiling; the chandelier crashed to the floor, narrowly missing Lieutenant Carstairs's head.

'Jamie, are you all right?'

Zoe was kneeling over him. He got to his feet. The sergeant who had been guarding them was dead; so was one of the soldiers. The room was full of men in all kinds of uniforms.

'The Doctor?' he said. 'They were going to shoot him.'

The Doctor's face appeared in the crowd. 'I'm safe and sound, Jamie. Zoe and her companions met up with this group of resistance fighters. The château is in our hands now.'

'The general,' said Jamie. 'He's in that little room over there. He'll be sending a message for help.'

'Come on, lads,' cried Sergeant Russell. 'Break down that door.'

Six men picked up one of the trestle tables. Using it as a battering ram, they ran at the bedroom door. The door caved in with a crash of splintering wood. Two shots were fired from inside the bedroom—the general was shooting at his attackers. One of the men who had battered down the door fell dead. The French soldier raised his rifle and fired once into the bedroom.

'You mustn't kill him,' cried the Doctor. 'He could tell us why ...'

The Doctor's words trailed off. He stood in the shattered doorway regarding the body of General Smythe, killed outright by a single shot through the forehead. Zoe came up behind the Doctor.

'Doctor, what's that?'

She pointed to a panel in the wall opposite the tele-communications unit. It too had been concealed, camouflaged by a section of the wall itself, now slid to one side.

'Some kind of control console,' said the Doctor, regarding the neat rows of buttons and knobs. He picked up a broken chair that lay immediately below the panel. 'I think he was trying to destroy it.' Marks were clearly visible on the panel where General Smythe had smashed at it with the chair. 'I wonder if it has something to do with creating the time zones?'

Zoe suddenly remembered. 'Doctor, that video screen!' She turned to look across to the other side of the room. The picture of the Royal Family was moved to one side and the video screen was glowing. She leapt across the little room and turned it off. 'They probably heard everything you said, Doctor.'

'It hardly matters,' he replied. 'You don't think they're going to leave us in peace very long, do you?'

Far away in the war room the Security Chief, War Chief and the War Lord saw the monitor screen go blank.

'Smythe was a fool,' said the War Chief. 'He deserved to die.'

'The processing machine head,' said the War Lord. 'Does this Doctor have the knowledge and ability to use it?'

'Yes,' said the War Chief. 'I believe he has.'

'Then the situation is urgent. Fortunately, though, they have made a very stupid mistake.' The War Lord waited to see which of his subordinates would ask what the mistake was. Neither was foolish enough to betray his own lack of imagination, so he continued. 'By carrying out a mass attack, they have concentrated resistance forces in one place—this château.'

'This time we should use our own guards,' said the Security Chief. 'I shall mount an invasion of the château by twenty sidrats. A hundred of our guards will emerge from each, their guns set to kill.'

The War Chief was appalled. 'You will invalidate the whole experiment! As the War Lord so wisely pointed out, they are all in one place. We can wipe them out with an artillery barrage.'

'Which,' said the War Lord, 'would be just as fool-hardy as using our security guards. Artillery would almost certainly destroy our control units there. Time zone barriers would vanish. In any case, let us not forget the purpose of the war games. We want battles. We need to know which of Earth's soldiers are the fiercest and can best be relied on to fulfil our destiny.'

The War Lord rose and went to the great war map. 'We shall order our human species to make a mass attack on the château. If they are British let them believe the Kaiser is there. If German, tell them this Doctor is the King of England. We shall mount a pincer movement with this Doctor and his group of bandits in its jaws!'

In flickering lamp-light Lieutenant Carstairs stood on a chair as he addressed the resistance fighters. In all kinds of ragged uniforms they had crowded into the château's one-time drawing room.

'You all know that some terrible trick is being played on us.'

The soldiers responded with an angry murmur.

'We are an elite, because for all of us in this room the trick has stopped working.' He paused while those who understood English translated his words into a variety of languages. 'What we must do now is to find other groups of resistance fighters so that together we can create one big army.'

It was during his second pause for translations that Sergeant Russell came hurrying through the shattered french windows. He pushed his way through the crowd to speak to Carstairs.

'Time's up for speech-making, sir. There's a whole British regiment coming up the road towards us. Our patrol has just spotted them.'

He had hardly finished giving his message when the French soldier came running in. In his excitement he cried out in French: *'M'sieur lieutenant, les boches avancent là-derrière vers le château!'* ('Lieutenant, the Germans are advancing towards the back of the château!')

A multilingual hubbub broke out among the soldiers. A young Russian officer of 1812 wielded his sword above the heads of those around him, causing most of them to duck. 'We must fight for our honour! We must die like heroes at the battle for Moscow!'

'You die like a hero,' growled a New Yorker from Abraham Lincoln's Unionist Army of the American Civil War. 'Lootenant, whyn't we get the hell out of here under the cover of darkness and re-group some-place else? That's make sense to me.'

'It does not make sense to me.' The Doctor spoke from the open door of the little room that had been General Smythe's bedroom. Heads turned towards him. 'We need to hold a firm base. There is important equipment here that may solve some of our problems.'

Carstairs looked down to Sergeant Russell. 'Do you think we could defend this place?'

'We can have a good try. What about it, lads?' the sergeant called to the crowd of soldiers.

'Ve have the advantage of darkness,' a German called back.

'I shall go into their ranks,' cried the 1812 Russian officer, 'slashing them to pieces with my sword. Only the dead will know that Boris Ivanovich Petrovich of the House of Trebetskoy has been among them.'

'Good on you, sport,' said an Australian infantry-man wearing a slouch hat. 'Let's get out of this room before they arrive. Otherwise we're sitting ducks.'

As Lieutenant Carstairs went into a strategy discussion with the sergeant and leaders of other resistance groups, the Doctor turned back into the little bedroom.

Zoe said, 'Do you really think you can make this gadget work, Doctor?' She sat on the edge of the camp bed looking at the control console in the wall.

'I can try,' he said. 'It's a question of how much time I've got before the château is overrun.'

The War Lord looked down at the war map. 'How are we progressing?'

The War Chief pointed to illuminated colours appearing on the map. 'British troops advancing here and here, converging with French troops. The Germans are pressing in on the rear of the château.'

'Good, good,' said the War Lord. 'A splendid manoeuvre.'

The War Chief smiled. 'Thank you.'

'But taking rather a long time,' said the Security Chief. 'Either our processed specimens aren't trying or these bandits are putting up a good fight.'

'They cannot win,' said the War Chief, still glowing from the War Lord's compliment. 'They will be crushed.'

'They've escaped before,' snarled the Security Chief. 'They could do it again. Do you intend the Doctor to die with the rest?'

'Why not?' asked the War Chief. 'He is now the main cause of our troubles.'

The Security Chief did not answer.

'Well?' said the War Lord. 'What did you mean by your question, Security Chief?'

The Security Chief could not evade answering the War Lord. 'The Doctor seems to have a charmed life that's all I meant.' He gave a respectful bow to the War Lord and moved away from the war map on the pretext of conferring with one of his security guards

The War Lord waited until the Security Chief was out of earshot. 'What was really behind his question about the fate of this Doctor?'

'He doesn't trust me,' the War Chief replied honestly. 'But I can assure you, War Lord, the Doctor will be killed. You have my word on it.' He glanced down at the war map where the illuminated colours had expanded. 'Look, your pincer movement has the château in its jaws! Time is running out for all those who resist us.'

The battle was raging all around the château now. Under pressure from the British regiment at the front of the building, resistance fighters had pulled back and were defending from the windows. Jamie and Sergeant Russell were crouched at a window, each with a rifle, firing whenever they could see a British steel helmet in the flash of explosions in the grounds.

'We should have done what that Yank said.' The sergeant aimed his rifle and fired. 'We should have pulled out of here and re-grouped somewhere else. Now it's too late.' He fired again.

From where Lieutenant Carstairs was firing his revolver he called, 'Watch that french window!'

One of the attackers, a young British corporal, had come right up to the window. Using his teeth he pulled out the pin of a hand grenade. He threw the grenade into the room.

'Why, you——' Sergeant Russell dropped his rifle and sprang at the corporal, grappling with him in hand to hand fighting. As the sergeant knocked out the corporal, Jamie threw himself at the grenade. In one movement he picked it up and hurled it back through the windows. It exploded outside with a blinding flash and a roar.

Carstairs ran to the little bedroom where the Doctor and Zoe were working. 'Doctor, they're starting to break in. We must either surrender or try to make a run for it under cover of darkness.'

'I don't think there is any need for either of those courses of action,' replied the Doctor. He made a finishing touch to his adjustments to the control console set in the wall. 'Now let's see if this thing can do what I want it to do.' He turned one of the control knobs. The console hummed with power.

'Doctor,' Carstairs pleaded, 'there's no time now to be fiddling with gadgets.'

'Isn't there? Then listen.'

Lieutenant Carstairs was about to speak again when he realised that the sound of battle had ceased. An eerie silence hung over the château.

'Doctor, what have you done?'

'I've set up a time zone barrier all around this building. That's what this gadget was for—to create and control those mists.'

'Don't you see,' said Zoe, enthusiastically, 'none of the processed soldiers will be able to get at us. But all of us will be able to move about freely.'

'By jingo,' said Carstairs. 'That's devilish ingenious.'

'Exactly what I thought,' said the Doctor, rising. 'The battle is now over.' He moved past Carstairs into the main room. 'Don't worry,' he announced to the astonished resistance fighters crouched at the windows. 'There'll be no more shooting tonight.' He noticed the young British corporal whom Sergeant Russell had knocked out. Jamie and the sergeant had tied the man's ankles and wrists. 'Who's he?'

'A brave lad,' said the sergeant. 'And a pity he's on the wrong side. He's our prisoner.'

'He's just the person I need,' said the Doctor. 'Quickly, get him untied and sit him on a chair.'

On the war map a bright red ring glowed all around the château.

'Smythe should have destroyed that apparatus as we ordered him,' said the War Chief.

'And we should have sent in my security guards,' said the Security Chief.

'Silence!' said the War Lord. 'I will not have this bickering. The use of human specimens to smash the bandits has failed. We must now take direct action. Security Chief, prepare a landing party.'

*

In the absence of the proper cowl, the Doctor had attached wires from the processing machine to a German steel helmet. Now he removed it from the head of the young British corporal. All the resistance fighters watched to see if the de-processing had worked. The Doctor snapped his fingers in front of the corporal's eyes.

'Come on,' he said sharply. 'What can you see?'

The young man looked around the motley group of soldiers. 'Where am I? Who are you all?'

'He seems pretty confused,' said Lieutenant Carstairs.

'Wouldn't you be,' responded the Doctor, 'if one moment you think you're fighting the Germans, and the next you know you're in a room surrounded by Turks, Russians, Frenchmen *and* Germans?' He turned back to the corporal. 'What can you remember?'

'I was on the Somme.' He smiled as he remembered some good news. 'The Americans have just declared war on the Kaiser. That means we can't lose now.' Confusion returned to his face. 'Then everything went funny. Have I been hit? Is this heaven?'

'This proves that machine works,' said Sergeant Russell. He grinned. 'But we're going to have to explain a lot to these fellows——'

The sound came from the bedroom. At first it was almost inaudible against the chatter of the exultant resistance fighters. By the time it had impinged on everyone's mind, the materialisation noise of the sidrat was almost complete.

'Take up positions of defence,' ordered Lieutenant Carstairs. 'Get these tables up as barricades!'

The soldiers scrambled to get the trestle tables across the floor to use as shields. A group of soldiers rushed to the bedroom door, firing their assorted rifles, shotguns and revolvers into the room. In return came the *zing* of stun-guns. Two men fell dead. All at once silver-uniformed security guards were coming through the door, firing their stun-guns indiscriminately. Three guards made straight for the Doctor, grabbing him before he had time to move.

'Don't shoot!' Jamie yelled. 'You'll hit the Doctor!'

The Doctor was dragged, kicking and struggling, into the bedroom. The security guards withdrew as quickly as they came. An Austro-Hungarian soldier raced to the bedroom door, fired a shot, and recoiled as he was hit by a stun-gun.

The sidrat's dematerialisation sound filled the whole château.

9

The Trap

The Security Chief looked down at his prisoner. The Doctor was securely strapped to a chair, the pain cowl over his head.

'Admit it,' said the Security Chief. 'Admit that the War Chief sent for you. You are both of the same race. Your arrival on this planet is part of a plot to betray us to the Time Lords!'

'You would never believe the truth,' said the Doctor. 'So I prefer to remain silent.'

'What you prefer doesn't matter.' The Security Chief signalled to a guard to turn on the power. 'Can you feel pain coursing through your head? Believe me, I can destroy your mind. When I have finished with you, you will be an imbecile.'

The door of the security room flew open. The War Chief and two of his bodyguards stepped in.

'Are you trying to kill him?' the War Chief demanded.

The Security Chief signalled for the power to be turned off. 'I'm trying to get the truth from him.'

'I congratulate you on the capture, but you will never make him talk that way. He is of my race. Your machines cannot work on us if we choose to resist.'

The Security Chief stepped back. 'You admit that you know him, War Chief?'

'Of course. And only I can deal with him. Release him. He's coming with me.'

'He is my prisoner.'

'And I am your superior. Get all that stuff removed, please.'

In silent outrage the Security Chief turned to the security guard. 'You heard what the War Chief said.'

The security guard removed the pain cowl and the straps.

'I shall question him in my own way in the war room,' said the War Chief. 'No doubt you will wish to report that to the War Lord the moment we have left this room.'

Escorted by the bodyguards the Doctor left the room followed by the War Chief. The Security Chief stood staring at the closed door, his face crimson with anger.

The War Chief took the Doctor into his private office just off the war room and told his bodyguards to leave.

'Now,' he said, 'a traveller in a time-space machine. There is only one person you can be.'

'I had every right to leave,' said the Doctor.

'And to steal a TARDIS?' The War Chief smiled. 'Not that I am criticising you. I left our people too. We are two of a kind.'

'We most certainly are not!' the Doctor protested.

The War Chief shrugged. 'Well, we were both Time Lords. Tell me, why did you decide to desert our kin?'

'I had reasons of my own. Rather different from yours, I imagine.'

'Probably they were. Why don't you sit down?' The War Chief settled himself into his own comfortable chair. 'How much have you learnt of our plans here?'

'Obviously you have kidnapped soldiers from various times in the history of the planet Earth, and you've brought them here to kill each other.'

The War Chief nodded. 'Very good observation. But do you realise our ultimate objective?'

'No objective can justify such slaughter,' said the Doctor.

'The war games on this planet are simply a means to an end,' the War Chief explained. 'The War Lords intend to conquer the entire galaxy. For this an army is needed not only of immense size but also of the utmost ferocity. Our purpose with these mock wars is to eliminate the cowards and the fools. We are only interested in recruiting the survivors.'

'How disgusting,' said the Doctor. 'But tell me, why

have you only abducted fighting men from the planet Earth?'

'Mankind is the most vicious species of all in the galaxy. Consider its history. Since they emerged from apes they have been systematically killing each other, either to gain land, or in the name of God, or for politics. We can turn the savage instincts of these humans to good purpose. We shall bring a new order of peace to the galaxy. And you can help.'

The Doctor eyed the War Chief. 'You have given these War Lords our knowledge and science to carry out this despicable scheme?'

'To create eternal peace, Doctor.'

'It sounds more like an empire of slaves.'

'With you and me in control.' The War Chief leant forward in his chair. 'Doctor, I am trying to save your life. If I can convince the War Lord that you will help us——'

He stopped short as the door opened. The War Lord entered followed by the Security Chief and his guards.

'Interrogation,' said the War Lord, 'is the business of the Security Chief.'

The War Chief stood up, but not so quickly as to suggest humility. 'I know this man. He is a fugitive Time Lord.'

'Like yourself,' said the War Lord. He turned to the Doctor. 'Have you informed the Time Lords of what we are doing?'

'He dare not,' said the War Chief. 'It would betray him.'

'He has allied himself with the resistance,' said the Security Chief. 'He has organised them against us. He must die.'

'On the contrary,' said the War Chief. 'He now knows that the resistance is futile. I have convinced him to join us. He can help us destroy the resistance.'

'He should be killed now,' the Security Chief insisted. 'We cannot possibly trust him.'

'Silence!' The War Lord paused to consider. 'If he helps us to destroy the resistance then his life will be spared. War Chief, I shall hold you personally responsible. Failure will mean death—for both of you.'

The War Lord turned and left the little office. After a moment's hesitation the Security Chief and his guards followed.

'I didn't promise to help you,' said the Doctor.

'I have just saved your life, Doctor. Show a little gratitude. You will help me because you have no alternative.'

'And help people like your new friends to conquer the galaxy? Never!'

The War Chief sat back again in his comfortable chair. 'Not people like that, Doctor. People like us. I intend to become the supreme ruler. Would you not like to share power with me?'

With dawn the resistance fighters at the château buried their dead and counted the wounded. The German soldier came down from the attic room where he had spent most of the night keeping watch on the surrounding land.

'Ze mist is still there. All soldiers are gone.' He slumped onto the floor, his back against the wall, exhausted. 'I see Sergeant Russell coming with Mexican man.' He fell fast asleep.

'My goodness,' said Lieutenant Carstairs. 'I wonder just how many wars they have going on in this place?'

During the night, search parties had been sent out to seek more resistance fighters. With the aid of Zoe's remarkable memory they had drawn up a list of people they wanted to contact.

Sergeant Russell arrived at the french windows with the Mexican. The newcomer wore a sombrero; his huge frame was bedecked with cartridge belts, knives, hand grenades and two holstered pearl-handled revolvers. In his fist he clutched a rifle.

'Arturo Villar,' Russell announced. 'He is holding two of our people outside the grounds as hostages in case this is a trick. His troops are surrounding the place.'

'Not troops,' said Villar in a strong Mexican accent. 'Bandits!' He grinned.

'Jolly glad to meet you,' said Lieutenant Carstairs. 'What war were you taken from?'

'Mexico,' said Villar. 'In Mexico is all war. The soldiers kill the peasants, we kill the soldiers. You wanna be my friends, huh?'

'We want you to be our friend,' said Zoe.

Villar looked at her, astonished. 'What kind of men are you? You let a girl speak for you.'

'She's one of us,' said Jamie. 'A fighting member of the resistance.'

At the sight of Jamie, Villar bellowed with laughter. 'A man in a woman's dress! You got no trousers to wear?'

'Tell me, Mr Villar,' said Carstairs. 'How many men can you contribute to the army we are creating?'

'Is secret. But plenty. All dirty fighters. Take no prisoners.' Villar ran his finger across his throat and laughed again.

'Are they a disciplined force?' asked Carstairs, persevering.

'Sure. They don't do what I say, I strangle them with my bare hands. They are plenty disciplined.'

'I think we'll find them useful,' said Sergeant Russell. 'We need everyone we can get. Perhaps we could tell Mr Villar our plan.'

'It's quite simple,' said Carstairs. 'We intend to make a mass attack on the base of the terrible people who have brought us all here. During the attack there is someone there that we must rescue.'

'Okay,' said Villar. 'You tell me where is this base, we go kill everyone.' He poised himself in the french window ready to go the moment someone told him where.

'It's not so simple,' said Carstairs. 'We can only get there in one of these boxes that appears and disappears. We know this château is one of the landing points, but we are surely under observation here.'

'There's another landing place we know,' said

Jamie. 'In a barn that's by a wood. We could assemble any number of soldiers under the cover of those trees.'

'I know that place,' said Boris Ivanovich Petrovich of the House of Trebetskoy. 'It's true—an army could hide there.' He sat on the floor nursing an arm wounded in last night's battle.

'This base,' said the French soldier. 'It will be well defended?'

'We have a plan to overcome that,' said Zoe. 'Lieutenant Carstairs, I think it's time you explained what we're going to do.'

The Roman officer stepped out of his tent, drew his cloak around him, and looked across the wide valley to the hill on the other side. Somewhere beyond the crest his human specimens should be slaughtering Ancient Britons; if not, the Ancient Britons were slaughtering the legionaries. It did not really matter. Only survivors interested him, humans who would soon form the War Lords' great army.

He heard a sound the other side of his tent and walked around it to see who was there. He found himself facing a German private of 1917 and an American from a New York regiment of 1862. The American, a sergeant, was holding a British service revolver.

'Hi!' said the American, seemingly affable.

It was the last word the fake Roman officer ever heard. The bullet from the revolver killed him outright.

The German and the American pulled aside the flap of the tent. Inside was an ornate wooden chest. The German took the dead officer's knife and prised open the lid.

'There it is,' said the American. They were looking down at a telecommunication unit.

The American emptied the revolver into the video screen.

Petrov Ilavich stood where his commander had told him to stand guarding the little hut. He had no idea what was inside the hut; only the commander ever went in there, and he did not talk with the ordinary soldiers.

Petrov wished the war was over so that he could be back with his father and mother on their little farm. He could no longer remember how long ago he had had to join the Tsar's army to fight the wicked British in the Crimea. Secretly he was thankful that no one had shot at him yet. Not once had he been in any fighting. His only duty had been to guard the commander's little hut. Yet this meant disgrace. For what could he boast of to his mother and his father when finally he went back home?

While these thoughts went through the mind of Petrov Ilavich, two other men from different wars were quietly placing dynamite sticks under the back of the hut. A Chinese soldier from the Boxer Rising of 1900 and one of Arturo Villar's Mexican bandits worked together, silently connecting the dynamite to wire on a drum. Once finished they ran with the drum to a boulder behind which they had placed the plunger. With deft movements, the Chinese made the final connection. He nodded to his Mexican companion. The Mexican grinned broadly and put his whole weight on top of the plunger.

The little hut disintegrated in a flash of flame and smoke. Whereas Petrov Ilavich had been standing upright at one moment, the next he was flat on his face with sections of wooden wall on top of him. Slowly he extricated himself, glad to find that none of his limbs was broken, and, even more important, he had not lost the Tsar's rifle. He stood up, brushing dust from his long grey coat. The hut had vanished. The commander would be furious. But it did not matter. At last Petrov Ilavich could claim to be a hero.

Another 'malfunction' light flashed up on the console in the war room.

'The Crimean War Zone,' said a technician, pointing excitedly.

'Two communication failures,' said the Security Chief. 'It's too much of a coincidence for these to be technical faults. Send a squad of guards to each.'

The technician was about to pass on the order when another 'malfunction' light flashed. 'Look, sir. First World War Zone, German front line.'

'Then to each point,' screamed the Security Chief, 'send a sidrat with a dozen guards. No, make it twenty guards to each. We must crush this insurrection!'

'Yes, sir,' said the technician. He passed on the order.

An officer of the 3rd South Carolina Regiment came rushing into the barn. He made straight for the stall containing the hidden communications unit. Arturo Villar, hot in pursuit, held his fire until the officer had revealed the video screen. Realising he was trapped, the panting officer wheeled round to face the men who had been chasing him.

'I am your commanding officer,' he gasped, doing his best to keep the steady monotone that would summon up loyalty from a processed human mind. 'You are not to shoot me because you are under my command. You are my faithful soldiers.'

'Oh, yes,' Villar guffawed. 'We are all very faithful, señor.' His two revolvers blazed at point blank range.

One of Villar's fellow bandits leapt forward to get at the fallen officer's pockets. Villar knocked the man to one side.

'You have no respect for the dead?' He laughed again. 'Then at least have respect for me. I take first choice!' With quick movements he stripped the dead officer of his cigar case, fob watch and Confederate money. The money he used to light cigars for all his group. A British soldier of 1917 stepped forward to fire into the video screen. Villar knocked the gun from the man's hand.

'Idiot! This one we must save. I think you English have little sense of the discipline, no?'

*

110

'I tell you, it's a clear pattern.' The Security Chief stood before a row of 'malfunction' lights. 'Attacks in every time zone.' He addressed his remarks to the War Lord, War Chief, and the Doctor.

'You have sent guards to deal with every attack on our communications units?' asked the War Chief.

'Of course!'

'So you have left our base open to a mass attack?' The War Chief smiled at the Security Chief's expense.

'Yes, but ...' The Security Chief turned to the War Lord. 'It's all happened so quickly. What else could I do?' A thought crossed his mind. 'Anyway, if there is to be a mass attack I know where it will come from. The American Civil War Zone. The communication was activated there by someone, but was not destroyed.'

'Knowing where an attack may come from,' said the War Lord, 'is militarily helpful. But how do you propose to deal with it if you have scattered guards all over the time zones?'

'That's very simple.' Before explaining, the Security Chief shot a glance at the Doctor. 'Why is he privy to our discussion? He's a prisoner. He should be locked up, or even better—dead.'

'I believe he is going to help us,' said the War Chief. 'What is this simple way whereby we can defend the main base?'

'The neutron bomb.'

'You'll wipe out every living thing,' said the War Chief. 'Have you gone mad?'

'The war games are over. Your experiment has been a total failure.'

'Because of your failure to provide proper security,' the War Chief retorted.

'This stupid rivalry must cease,' said the War Lord angrily. 'There is a way to crush the resistance once and for all.' He looked at the Doctor. 'If you really want to join us, this will be an opportunity for you to prove your new loyalty.' He paused. 'You do want to join us, don't you?'

'Do I have any option?' asked the Doctor.

'Of course you have,' replied the War Lord. 'I am not one to force a man to do something against his nature. If you prefer to remain our enemy I shall simply kill you.'

Lieutenant Carstairs, Sergeant Russell, Zoe and Jamie, and all the resistance leaders they had managed to find, came into the barn.

'Salud,' said Arturo Villar by way of welcome. He flicked ash from his cheroot onto the body of the officer from the 3rd South Carolina Regiment. 'Now we are all together,' he said. 'What a target we make, huh?'

'It's the plan,' Jamie reminded him. 'How many men have you got outside?'

'Plenty men,' said Villar. 'You all got plenty men?'

'Twenty-five cossacks awaiting my command,' announced Boris Ivanovich Petrovich of the House of Trebetskoy.

'I do not disclose to anyone the size of my force,' said a 1917 German officer in perfect English. 'But it is considerable.'

'Altogether we've got some hundreds of resistance soldiers waiting in the woods,' said Carstairs. 'The sooner we get one of those boxes to appear, the better. Here goes!' He raised his revolver, aimed point blank at the video screen, and thumbed back the hammer. To his astonishment the Doctor's face appeared on the screen.

'Don't shoot,' said Zoe. 'He must know we're here and wants to speak to us.'

'But if he's a prisoner . . .' Carstairs lowered his gun. 'Dashed if I can understand it.'

'Zoe?' said the Doctor. 'Jamie? Are you there in the barn?'

'Yes, Doctor,' said Jamie. 'Have you escaped?'

The Doctor spoke quietly. 'I have managed to gain control of their transportation system. Is Sergeant Russell with you?'

'Right here,' said Russell.

'All the resistance leaders are with us,' Zoe explained. 'We've got an army here, Doctor. Can you send us one of those machines to get us to the base?'

'Yes, I can.' They saw the Doctor glance over his shoulder, as though expecting to be interrupted by someone any moment. 'But all I need is a hand-picked force. I need to meet all the leaders.'

'Wouldn't it be safer if we sent as many men as possible?' Jamie asked.

'No, Jamie.' A note of urgency had crept into the Doctor's voice. 'Just do as I say. I shall send you transport immediately.'

The screen went blank.

'I don't like this,' said Villar. 'It could be a trap. Maybe somebody hold a gun on him.'

'He wouldn't lie to us,' said Jamie.

The barn reverberated to the sound of a sidrat materialising. Some of the resistance leaders unaccustomed to the sound looked alarmed.

'There is nothing to worry about,' Carstairs said loudly. 'But everyone take cover in case there are guards to deal with.'

Within moments everyone had ducked out of sight. The sidrat appeared in exactly the same spot as before. Its door opened.

'Keep your heads down,' Carstairs ordered from behind a bale of hay. 'Let me check.' He walked forward, gun in hand, and looked into the sidrat. 'It seems to be empty.'

'Of course it is,' said Jamie. 'The Doctor wouldn't send one with those stun-gun men.'

The resistance leaders emerged from their hiding places. Some went up to the sidrat to touch it, still not believing what they had seen.

'One of us should stay behind,' said Sergeant Russell, 'to be in charge of those men out in the forest.' He turned to Boris Ivanovich. 'How about you?'

'I prefer always to attack,' said the 1812 Russian. 'I shall slice the enemy with my sabre.'

'Mine is the biggest group,' said Arturo Villar. 'I stay here in charge.'

'Why?' said Sergeant Russell. 'Are you scared of going into that thing?'

Villar pulled himself up to his full height. 'Arturo Villar is scared of nothing!'

'Then in you go.'

Villar looked from one to another of the people around him. He was trapped by his own pride.

'I shall lead the way,' he announced. Concealing his fears of the extraordinary contraption, he marched into the sidrat. All the other resistance leaders, except the Russian, followed. The door closed and the sidrat quickly dematerialised.

Boris Ivanovich stood scratching his chin. To him the appearance and disappearance of the sidrat was not science, for he knew nothing of science. It was magic, and that he could understand better. The magician was obviously the Doctor, whose talking image had appeared so mysteriously in the mirror on the wall at the back of the stall.

How did the Doctor know they were all assembled in the barn? Boris Ivanovich wondered. But of course, a magician must know everything.

The Doctor stood alone waiting for the sidrat to materialise. As the door opened Lieutenant Carstairs was the first to step out.

'Doctor,' he said with genuine pleasure. 'How good to see you again.'

The Doctor was stern-faced. 'Where are the resistance leaders?'

'All here. They've been wandering around the halls and corridors inside this thing, amazed by its size. Here they are.'

Jamie, Zoe, Sergeant Russell, Arturo Villar and the other resistance leaders came out from the sidrat.

'It is fantastic,' said Villar, looking around the metal walls of the sidrat materialisation area. 'Who do I shoot?'

'No one yet,' replied the Doctor. 'Everyone follow me. We must occupy the war room. The whole base will then be in our hands.'

He led the group down a corridor. At an inter-
section silver-uniformed guards appeared, stun-guns
aimed at the group. With thoughts of a quick retreat,
Carstairs looked back. Behind the group guards filled
the corridor. The Doctor continued to walk forward
and the guards made way for him. Soon he was behind
them and had been joined by the War Chief and the
Security Chief.

'Do not try to resist,' he called to those who had
followed him from the sidrat. 'You are completely surrounded.'

'Doctor,' Zoe cried out, 'what's happened?'

'He has betrayed us,' said Carstairs bitterly.

The War Chief patted the Doctor's shoulder. 'Thank
you, Doctor. You have grought us a neat little package
to dispose of.'

10

Fall of the War Chief

The War Chief addressed the security guards at either end of the corridor. 'Take their guns!'

Guards moved into the group, taking rifles and pistols.

'I shall kill him,' said Villar. 'The Doctor I shall stake out in the sun and leave him to the ants. I shall bury him up to his neck and ride my horses over his head!'

'I don't understand the situation,' said Lieutenant Carstairs. 'You seemed a perfectly decent chap, Doctor. What's made you change sides in this reprehensible manner?' As he spoke a security guard relieved Carstairs of his revolver.

'We were idiots to trust him,' said Sergeant Russell. 'If we ever get out of this alive, Doctor, I'm going to——'

'Silence!' The War Chief's voice boomed down the corridor. 'If you prove to be courageous fighters none of you will be killed. But you are going to be re-processed, and there's nothing you can do about it.' He raised his voice again. 'Take them all away.'

'Take him, too,' the Security Chief said.

A security guard moved in on the Doctor, stun-gun raised.

'No,' protested the War Chief. 'He is working for us now.'

'He's done his job,' objected the Security Chief. 'He's no further use.'

'He has great knowledge of time travel mechanics, Security Chief.' The War Chief's voice was firm. 'He is now my personal assistant.'

The Security Chief wavered. 'The War Lord shall decide his fate.' He swung round to his guards. 'Get these prisoners to the processing room. If any try to escape, shoot to kill.' He turned back to the War Chief. 'I shall speak with the War Lord now about this special prisoner of yours.' He stalked off down the corridor.

The Doctor waited until the disarmed prisoners had been herded away before saying, 'Why do you so obviously need me?'

'We surely need each other,' said the War Chief.

'It's something to do with your travel machines, isn't it?'

'How intelligent of you,' said the War Chief. 'The sidrats that I designed for the War Lords have a limited life. The green crystal, which is the basis of our time control units, is unobtainable anywhere in the galaxy except on our planet of the Time Lords. For these sidrats I have had to use other materials. In time they will all wear out.'

'Now I understand,' said the Doctor. 'It's my TARDIS that you want. But surely you have one of your own?'

The War Chief smiled. 'No more mine than yours is really yours! We are both thieves, Doctor. Yes, I do have a TARDIS hidden away. But are not two better than one? While I rest and enjoy the spoils of victory, you can patrol our empire. And I shall do the same for you.'

'*Our* empire?'

'We shall rule the galaxy without fear of opposition,' the War Chief said confidently. 'For we shall be the only two who can travel through both space *and* time.'

A voice spoke from concealed loudspeakers. *'War Chief and his prisoner to report to the War Lord immediately!'*

'No doubt my dear friend the Security Chief stirring up trouble,' said the War Chief. 'Shall we go? It wouldn't do to keep the War Lord waiting.'

'You have done well,' said the War Lord. 'Yet your sudden decision to join us worries me.'

The Security Chief nodded smugly. 'Exactly my point, sir.'

'I have heard your side of the argument,' said the War Lord. 'Now let me hear theirs.' He looked to the Doctor to answer.

'I like to be on the winning side,' said the Doctor. 'The resistance has no chance against your might and power.'

The War Lord looked pleased by the compliment. 'Like your friend, the War Chief, you have a silver tongue. But now that we have the resistance leaders in our hands, what contribution can you make?'

'I could make your processing machines work effectively. Ask your scientist.'

'He is on our home planet,' said the War Lord, 'producing a new and better machine.'

'Given the chance,' said the Doctor, 'I can make the old one work with a hundred per cent success.'

The War Lord considered. 'You will have the opportunity to prove your skill. You will adjust the existing machines and re-process your resistance friends.'

'They are losers,' said the Doctor. 'They are no friends of mine!'

'Of course,' said the War Lord. He turned to the Security Chief. 'Take him to the processing room and give him every facility.'

The Doctor was alarmed at the prospect of being in the Security Chief's care. 'But, sir——'

'Have no fear,' said the War Lord. 'The Security Chief will carry out my orders and give you all the protection you need.' He gave a signal for the Security Chief and the Doctor to depart.

'Now,' said the War Lord to the War Chief. 'These resistance groups. What is the position?'

The War Chief pointed to the war map. 'They are all in this one area. I have ordered our human specimens to move in on them.'

'To capture or to kill?' asked the War Lord.

'To capture if possible,' replied the War Chief. 'Once re-processed we have good fighting men there for our eventual conquest of the galaxy.'

'Good, good,' said the War Lord. 'Let us never lose sight of the eventual aim. As soon as that's done we need all security guards returned to this base. All communications units are to be repaired or replaced and the war games are to continue.' The War Lord rose. 'I shall retire to my chamber now. Very soon we must start selecting the survivors of our games, War Chief. We must put them into storage for the great mission of galactic conquest that is to come!'

The prisoners stood waiting in the processing room, surrounded by silver-uniformed guards.

'They will shoot us,' said Villar. 'What else you do with prisoners, huh?'

'No,' said Lieutenant Carstairs. 'they will re-process us and send us back to fight their wars. Still, I suppose that comes to the same thing. The average length of life of a British officer at the front line is only three weeks.'

'Sir,' said Sergeant Russell, quietly, 'shouldn't we be trying to break out of here?'

Carstairs looked at the armed guards. 'With that lot on top of us?' He turned to Jamie. 'You've always seemed a decent young fellow. Who is this Doctor really?'

Jamie was at a loss to answer. 'He's ... well, he can travel through time and space. I don't really know.'

Zoe said, 'I don't like the way he seems to know that War Chief. It's as though they had some bond——'

The door opened. The Security Chief pushed the Doctor into the room. 'Let's see what you can do with these prisoners, Doctor. Prove what you promised to the War Lord.'

The Doctor was hesitant. 'I shall do my best.'

'Good,' said the Security Chief. 'Unfortunately, I cannot spare all these guards to protect you from your friends. You will have to fend for yourself. Guards— outside!'

The half dozen security guards left the room. The Security Chief remained at the door. 'Turn them all into docile specimens for our war games, Doctor. I shall return later—much later.' He stepped out of the room and closed the door.

The Doctor swung round to open the door. It was locked. He turned to the prisoners, his back to the door. 'There are certain things you should understand,' he started to say.

'We understand,' said Arturo Villar. 'First I kill you with my bare hands, then I listen.'

Villar lunged at the Doctor, hands reaching for his neck. Jamie made a cross tackle, pushing Villar away, while Zoe took up a position in front of the trapped Doctor.

'You want I should kill you first?' thundered Villar. He laughed unpleasantly. 'I never kill a man before wearing a skirt!'

'I don't think anyone should kill anyone,' said Carstairs. 'But Doctor, I think you owe us an explanation.'

'Thank you,' said the Doctor. 'I am trying to save your lives. They were going to use the neutron bomb, and that would have killed every human on this planet. This way we still have a chance. If you do exactly as I say, you will come to no harm.'

Villar thrust Jamie aside. 'We don't listen to no more lies! We execute the traitor!'

Pushing Zoe out of his way, Villar successfully grabbed at the Doctor's throat. Zoe rained blows onto Villar's back that he did not seem to notice. Jamie tugged at his arms.

'This is plain murder,' stormed Lieutenant Carstairs. He appealed to the resistance leaders. 'Help me stop this madman.'

Sergeant Russell shook his head. 'No, sir. This is justice——'

The door flung open. Two armed guards entered with the War Chief.

'Stop!' he roared. He nodded to one of the guards who prodded Villar away from the Doctor with a stungun. 'I apologise, Doctor, for this misunderstanding.'

'It was almost fatal.' The Doctor straightened his clothes, ruffled by Villar's manhandling. 'Perhaps now I may proceed with my contribution to the success of your plans.'

'Our plans,' said the War Chief. 'You're one of us now.'

Jamie was the first to be processed.

'You're quite sure,' asked the War Chief, 'that with your adjustments to the machine the process will be total?'

'The basic principles of your process were sound,' said the Doctor, busying himself with controls on the humming machine, 'but there were certain defects in the application. I happen to know more about the working of the human mind than your scientist.' He checked the dials again and then turned the machine off. The humming stopped. 'This young man should now believe himself to be fighting English redcoats in 1745 Earth time.' He raised his voice to address Jamie. 'What is your name?'

'James Robert Macrimon. But you know ...'

'And where are you?' the Doctor cut in.

'I ...'

'You are in my castle,' said the Doctor. 'I am the Macrimon of Macrimon, your hereditary chieftain.'

Jamie looked up at the Doctor rather dubiously. 'Aye, that's right. Who's that?' He pointed to the War Chief.

'A friendly chieftain. You will obey his orders as you would mine.' The Doctor indicated Zoe, Carstairs and the resistance leaders, whom the War Chief's guards had lined up to await processing. 'Those are members of our clan.'

Jamie tried to rise up, an accusing finger directed at Carstairs. 'He's an Englishman! A redcoat!'

Unseen by the War Chief, the Doctor kicked Jamie's ankle. 'Kidnapped by the English, brought up to speak in the Sassenach way, but by blood a true Highlander.'

Jamie subsided. 'That's all right then.'

'Excellent,' said the War Chief. 'Continue with the others. If you can process characters like these you will have made an immense contribution. I shall go to tell the War Lord of your success.'

'You will leave some of your guards here?' asked the Doctor, nervously.

'Have no fear, Doctor. This time you will be protected.' The War Chief left the processing room.

'You are next,' said the Doctor, pointing at Zoe. 'Take your place in the machine.'

Since Zoe did not respond instantly, a guard grabbed her arm and yanked her forward.

'You've no right to do this,' she screamed. 'Leave me alone!'

'It's for your own good,' said the Doctor. 'You must obey my orders completely.'

Behind the guard's back, the Doctor winked.

The War Chief entered the war room.

'Is the War Lord here?' he asked.

The Security Chief turned from the telecommunications console. 'Guards to position,' he ordered.

Security guards closed in behind the War Chief.

'What is the meaning of this?' he demanded. 'A joke?'

'Listen,' said the Security Chief. He activated a small control on the console. The war room was filled with a recording of the Doctor's voice.

'And help people like your new friends to conquer the galaxy? Never!'

It was followed by the War Chief's response.

'Not people like that, Doctor, People like us. I intend to become the supreme ruler. Would you not like to share power with me?'

'I had your private office wired up,' said the Security Chief. 'Your entire conversation with your accomplice is on record, which I intend to play to the War Lord.'

The War Chief tried to say, 'I am your superior——'

'No more! You are not of our people. You have never had true loyalty to our cause! Guards, take this traitor to the security room. Collect the Doctor on the way. If they resist, kill them both.'

The guards closed in on the War Chief. One of them took his personal stun-gun.

The resistance leaders stood in line, eyes glazed like zombies.

'The last one,' the Doctor said to the security guards. 'Put him to the machine.'

A guard prodded Arturo Villar.

'For this I kill you, slowly,' Villar threatened. 'You do things to my mind, I do things to your throat.'

'You will feel nothing,' the Doctor explained. 'But if you do not co-operate like the others have done, the guard will shoot you dead.'

Villar looked down at the stun-gun pointing at his side. 'What can I do? I am defenceless.' He sat down.

The Doctor attached the helmet and made the necessary adjustments. Then he turned on the machine. It hummed loudly for ten seconds. He turned the control to 'off'.

'There,' he said. 'You are in La Castille de la Cruz de San Antonio, in Mexico.'

Villar looked round. 'Are you crazy? I am here in this room with all these people you make into imbeciles.' He rose up. 'Your machine is no good. Arturo Villar is too strong for you!'

He made a mighty lunge at the Doctor, hands open to take the Doctor's throat. The two guards left by the War Chief rushed forwards to grab Villar, turning their backs on the resistance leaders. It was the moment they had been waiting for.

'Now!' shouted Lieutenant Carstairs.

The group moved as one man to overpower the guards. They had no time to turn their stun-guns onto their attackers. The guards fell under a hail of blows from all sides. Ignoring what was happening, the single-minded Villar had the Doctor by the throat and was trying to strangle him.

'Help,' screamed the Doctor, trying to make his voice heard over the hubbub.

Jamie and Sergeant Russell pounced on Villar's back, dragging him from the Doctor.

'You great loon,' said Jamie. 'Couldn't you pretend like the rest of us?'

Villar looked around and then down at the fallen security guards. 'Is all a trick? The Doctor fix the machine so she doesn't work?'

'Yes,' said the Doctor, trying to get his breath. 'I fix the machine.'

Zoe had gone to the door to look out. She signalled frantically to the group. 'That War Chief and two guards are coming!'

'Everybody back as they were,' said Carstairs. To Villar and Sergeant Russell he added, 'Except you two. Cover the door.'

All the resistance leaders, with Jamie and Zoe, lined up as they had been before, affecting the vacant expressions of processed human specimens. The doctor returned to the machine and pretended to be concentrating on making a minor adjustment.

The door opened and the War Chief was pushed inside. One of the two guards stepped forward.

'You,' he said to the Doctor, 'come with us.'

Villar and Sergeant Russell struck simultaneously, felling the two guards with blows to the back of the neck. The War Chief looked round, startled.

'Don't harm him,' said the Doctor. 'I think we may need him.'

'More we need our guns,' said Villar. He turned on the War Chief, gripping him by the throat. 'I strangle him, he tell us where our guns are!'

'For goodness' sake,' said Lieutenant Carstairs, 'do stop throttling people, old man. Will you say where our guns are hidden?'

The War Chief, his face going blue, nodded. Villar let go of his throat.

'And will you help us gain control of the war room?' the Doctor asked.

The War Chief gingerly fingered his neck where Villar had half strangled him. 'That may not be easy.

Our arrangement was discovered. I came here under arrest. However, the technician in the sidrat landing bay doesn't know that. I could stop the arrival of the sidrats bringing back the guards you so cunningly drew out to the time zones.'

'Good,' said the Doctor. 'But first, before all else, you must come with us to the war room to stop the war games. This frightful slaughter must cease immediately.'

'First,' Villar insisted, 'we get back our guns—no?'

'No,' said the Doctor. 'I mean, yes. Come along.'

The Security Chief stood at the communications console speaking into a microphone. 'This is the Security Chief. The resistance forces, now leaderless, concentrated in the 1862 time zone, will be dealt with by armies of human specimens. Meanwhile, all security guards are to proceed to the nearest control point——'

He heard the grunt of a guard knocked out by Sergeant Russell and wheeled around. He was looking straight into the barrels of Villar's two six-shooters.

'Guards!' he screamed. 'Emergency alarm!'

The technician at the communications console just had time to press the emergency alarm button before Villar shot him in the back. Two guards the far side of the war room raised their stun-guns and were killed by rifle fire from the resistance leaders.

The Security Chief tried to unholster his own stun-gun, but the War Chief had already picked up the weapon dropped by the first guard to fall. With a single movement he adjusted the gun to 'kill', aimed at the Security Chief and fired. The *zing* on the stun-gun was immediately followed by the Security Chief's death scream.

Throughout, a high-pitched blast had emitted from loudspeakers in all the walls. 'Please turn that hideous thing off,' shouted the Doctor. 'I cannot think.'

The War Chief crossed to the communications console, stepping over the body of his rival, the Security Chief, and touched a control. The emergency alarm stopped.

'We've won,' said Sergeant Russell. 'We've got control!'

A little jubilant cheer went up from the motley assortment of resistance leaders—French, German, American, Roman, from all periods in history. A Greek and a Turk linked arms and began to dance.

'We haven't won yet,' said Zoe. 'Doctor, how are you going to get all these people back to their own times?'

'First things first, Zoe.' The Doctor turned to the War Chief. 'Stop the war games.'

All eyes were on the War Chief. 'I am a man of my word,' he said. He went to the microphone which the Security Chief had been using a few minutes earlier. 'This is the War Chief speaking. All hostilities in all time zones are to cease immediately. Officers are to tell their human specimens that an armistice has been declared. Further orders will be issued to you shortly.'

'That's a good start,' said Jamie. 'Now, Doctor, about getting these people back where they came from?'

'Can you return them the same way you brought them here?' asked the Doctor.

The War Chief shook his head. 'For journeys of such time and distance the life-spans of the sidrats are spent. I told you, Doctor, they are not like a real TARDIS.'

Sergeant Russell pushed forward in the crowd. 'You can't keep your promise, Doctor? We're stuck here?'

'There are people who can help us,' said the Doctor. 'The Time Lords.' He turned to Jamie. 'My own race. Now you know who I really am.'

'No!' said the War Chief. 'You mustn't call them! You know what will happen to us.'

'There is no alternative,' said the Doctor. 'Who is more important? The two of us or those tens of thousands of poor soldiers stranded on this planet? Please, all of you, keep quiet.'

The Doctor sat down cross-legged on the floor, fished

about in his capacious pockets and brought out six square metal plates. These he placed in a pattern on the floor before him.

'Doctor, please, I implore you,' said the War Chief.

'He told us to keep quiet,' said Jamie. 'That includes you!'

As the Doctor passed into a deep trance, the onlookers could hear a babble of whispering voices coming from the little squares of metal. Then, to their amazement, the squares began to move. They raised themselves from the floor and formed a perfect little box.

'Doctor,' said Zoe, 'are you all right? What's that thing?'

'A very special box,' said the Doctor. 'From my mind I have passed into it information about what has been going on here, and an appeal for help.'

'You've never asked for help before,' Jamie reminded him.

'The task of returning these men to their own time is too great for me.' The Doctor looked up. 'Believe me, War Chief, what we are doing is right——'

But there was only a gap where the War Chief had been standing, in the ring of people around the Doctor.

'He must have slipped out,' said Sergeant Russell, 'while we were all watching your magic tricks.'

'I don't blame him,' said the Doctor. 'I suggest we do exactly the same thing.' He got to his feet, picked up the box and popped it into his pocket. 'The sooner we get away from here the better.'

The War Chief approached the sidrat materialisation area cautiously. No one was about. He adjusted the controls of the console; instantly the area was filled with the sound of a sidrat arriving. When it finally appeared, he touched the control for its door to open.

'One moment,' said the voice.

He spun round. He was facing the War Lord and two armed guards who had quietly come down the corridor. His mouth suddenly went dry as he tried to think how to explain himself.

'War Lord, sir,' he said. 'I thought ...'

'Yes?'

'There's been a revolt. Prisoners escaped. I thought you'd been murdered in your private chamber.'

'Really?' said the War Lord. 'Then you should be pleased to see me alive. If so much is going on here, why are you making off in a sidrat?'

The War Chief thought quickly. 'To return to our home planet and bring back reinforcements. I intended to crush the revolt.'

'I see. How commendable. Where is the Security Chief?'

'The prisoners killed him. I tried to stop them. I'm lucky to have got away with my own life.' The War Chief edged towards the waiting sidrat.

'You are lying,' said the War Lord. 'He played to me the recording of your intended treachery. You killed him, but you killed him too late.'

'That recording was a forgery,' the War Chief spluttered. 'I can explain everything.'

The War Lord pointed his finger directly at the War Chief. 'Kill!'

Both guards fired together. Screaming, the War Chief fell at the open door of the sidrat.

'Remove that traitor's carcass,' the War Lord ordered. 'We shall return to our home planet and bring back sufficient of our own guards to quell this uprising once and for all!'

As the guards put down their stun-guns to deal with the War Chief's body, the War Lord went to the console to set the sidrat on a course to his home planet.

The resistance leaders crept quietly down the corridor leading into the sidrat area. Their stealth was broken by a sudden cry from the Mexican.

'Viva Villar!' he cried, brandishing his two revolvers.

Both guards dived for their abandoned stun-guns, and were cut down in a hail of revolver and rifle bullets. Villar rushed up to the War Lord, grabbed him by the throat and pushed the muzzle of a gun in his mouth.

'I squeeze the trigger?' he asked. 'Blow his head off?'

'Leave him for the Time Lords,' said the Doctor. 'They'll dispose of him.'

'I could break his neck with my two hands,' said Villar. 'Save a bullet, no?'

'Please be a good chap,' said Carstairs, 'and do as the Doctor suggests.'

Villar reluctantly released his choking prisoner.

'I am afraid,' said the Doctor, 'this is when I must leave you. The Time Lords have been summoned and will be here soon. They will return you all to your times in Earth's history.'

'Nice to have met you all,' said Jamie, standing now at the open door of the sidrat. 'Come on Zoe, it's back to the TARDIS.'

'No,' said the Doctor. 'You don't understand. You two must return to your right times in the past and the future.'

'But why, Doctor?' said Zoe. 'We're your friends. We want to stay with you.'

'From now on,' said the Doctor, 'I must travel alone. I may have to go to the farthest reaches of the universe. You two belong where I found you.'

'He is afraid,' said the War Lord. 'Afraid of the vengeance of his own people!'

'If you're in trouble,' said Jamie, 'I'm going to be there to help you.' He stepped past the Doctor into the sidrat.

'Me too,' said Zoe, following Jamie inside. 'If you don't want us you'll have to throw us out of this thing!'

The Doctor looked at their set, earnest faces. 'All right. But don't say I didn't warn you. We'll return to the 1917 zone where we left the TARDIS.'

Lieutenant Carstairs stepped forward. 'May I come along, too? It's my time zone and I'd like to try and find Lady Jennifer if I can.'

'Very well.' The Doctor stepped into the sidrat.

'Goodbye, gentlemen. You will all be home soon.'

The door of the sidrat snapped shut. The dematerialisation took only moments.

'I hope he was telling the truth,' said Sergeant Russell. 'We'll be in a fine mess if these Time Lords don't turn up.'

A sudden cold wind rushed through the corridors, subsiding as quickly as it came. The War Lord shivered.

'Have no fear,' he said. 'The Time Lords are on their way.'

Lieutenant Carstairs looked around the desolation of mud, barbed wire and waterlogged shell holes. 'It's so quiet.'

'The fighting has stopped,' said the Doctor.

Carstairs grabbed the Doctor's arm. 'Quick, into a shell hole!'

About two kilometres away the Doctor saw two men in grey uniforms with spiked helmets. 'No, Lieutenant, the fighting is over. You're not fighting Germans and they are not fighting you.'

'I'm sorry. How stupid of me.' Carstairs hesitated before putting his question. 'Doctor, did my war really end in 1917?'

'You mustn't ask me that, Lieutenant.'

'Then I can't ask whether my side won, or if I was killed?'

From a hillock of mud some distance away Jamie waved excitedly. He cupped his hands to his mouth and called across the wasteland. 'Over here, Doctor! I can just see it.'

'Excuse me,' said the Doctor, offering his hand. 'They have found my TARDIS. I must hurry.'

'Did my side win?' asked Carstairs, gripping the Doctor's hand. 'Was all the death and misery for nothing?'

'You have answered your own question, Lieutenant. War is always death and misery, and both sides lose. I hope that one day you humans will find another way to settle your arguments.'

The Doctor released his hand, and with a wave sped across the mud towards Jamie. A cold breeze suddenly whined across No Man's Land, chilling him to the bone. He put on greater speed to reach the top of the hillock where Jamie was waiting. Zoe was down the other side, urging them on.

'This way,' she called up to them. 'Not far to go.'

The TARDIS stood exactly where the Doctor had left it. The sight of it urged him on. Soon all three were racing across flat open land and the Doctor was already fishing in his pockets for the key.

Zoe, running ahead, was the first to hit the force field. All at once she was struggling against something unseen, like a swimmer in thick treacle.

'Doctor,' she called back, 'what's happening?'

'We must concentrate,' the Doctor gasped. 'Help me with the key.'

With a combined effort they managed to put the key in the lock of the TARDIS.

'We'll be all right now,' said Jamie.

But Zoe had already gone inside. 'No, it's in here. I can hardly breathe. It's ... it's drowning us.'

Outside another sudden gust of cold wind whipped across the land, and this time it kept blowing.

11

The Trial of Doctor Who

The Doctor struggled towards the control column and managed to pull the door lever. Once the door had closed their sense of drowning eased a little. The Doctor went to the dematerialisation controls.

'Let's see if I can boost enough power to break out of this force field. Hold on!'

The TARDIS shuddered, the sensation they were accustomed to when it took flight. All three sank to the floor, exhausted.

'We've made it,' said Jamie. 'We're on our way to—somewhere.' He knew from past experience the Doctor's inability to direct the TARDIS.

Zoe asked, 'Doctor, why are you trying to get away from the Time Lords? Why did you leave them in the first place?'

'I was bored. They're very dull. They have immense powers, their life spans are infinite. Yet all they do is to observe and gather knowledge. As for myself, I like to get involved in things.'

'You certainly do,' said Jamie with feeling.

Zoe said, 'Does the TARDIS belong to them?'

'What? Oh, I suppose it does in a sense.'

'You mean you stole it?'

'I borrowed it,' said the Doctor evasively. 'In any case, it's not one of the best models. The chameleon effect doesn't work. It shouldn't stay looking like a London police box, you know. It should always change to fit into its surroundings.'

'You still have no right to it,' said Zoe.

'Well, I suppose if one wanted to be very legalistic about the matter ...'

Fortunately for the Doctor, who did not wish to

pursue this conversation, the sound and shudder of materialisation started.

'That was quick,' said Jamie.

'I boosted the power,' said the Doctor. 'Let's see where we are.' He got up, crossed to the external scanner and turned it on. They saw a picture of beautiful flowers and lush foliage. 'Excellent! A galactic South Sea island.' He pulled the door lever. Brilliant sunshine flooded in.

Jamie stepped outside, breathing the sweet air. 'It's a bit better than No Man's Land!'

Zoe and the Doctor joined Jamie outside. 'How far have we travelled?' she asked.

'Trillions of light years, my dear. Don't worry, no one will find me here.'

As the words left his lips a gust of cold wind blew through the exotic flowers and foliage that surrounded them.

'No one, Doctor?' Zoe clutched his sleeve to pull him back to the TARDIS. 'That force field,' she exclaimed. 'I can feel it again, swamping me ...'

Pushing against the force they tumbled back into the TARDIS and the Doctor closed the door. He thrust the controls into dematerialisation overdrive. The floor shuddered.

'Where to now, Doctor?' asked Jamie.

'I've set the controls at random. Maybe that will shake them off.'

The floor had no sooner stopped shuddering from dematerialisation than it was shuddering again as they materialised.

'This is impossible,' said the Doctor. 'Surely we can't be landing again already?'

Zoe was first to the scanner. 'We're by the sea,' she said, looking at a picture she thought was from the shore looking across water. 'No we're not—we're *in* the sea!' The scanner had sunk below the water now. A shark swam by, pausing a few seconds to inspect the strange object before passing on.

'We'll sit it out below water,' said the Doctor. 'We

have all the air and food we need for as long as we like.'

A drop of water fell onto the control panel with a plop. As they turned to look another drop fell.

'It's the Time Lords,' said the Doctor. 'They have no sense of fair play. They are deliberately weakening the defence system. But there's one place we shall be safe, if I can get us there!' He rushed to the controls. This time there was no gap at all between the shudders of dematerialisation and materialisation.

'Where are we now?' asked Jamie.

'Outer Space,' announced the Doctor. 'There's a chance they'll lose track of us here.'

A voice boomed from all the walls of the TARDIS. 'There is no escape. Return the TARDIS immediately to our home planet. You have broken our laws. You must face your trial.'

'Oh, very well,' said the Doctor. 'If you insist.' He returned his attention to the controls.

'You're going to give in?' said Zoe.

'Sometimes, Zoe,' he said in a submissive voice, 'a run-away Time Lord has to know when he's beaten.' With a big wink to her, his hands leapt all over the control panel, frantically turning on sufficient power to escape from the Time Lords. The TARDIS shuddered violently, heaving from side to side like a small ship in a raging sea. The trio were thrown in all directions.

'What have you done?' cried Jamie.

'I've put it on maximum power-drive. It's our only chance.'

'It's shaking itself to pieces,' Zoe moaned, clinging on to the base of the control unit. 'Turn down the power, Doctor, or we'll all be killed.'

'You're right, Zoe.' Exerting great effort the Doctor raised himself to the controls. He stared at the levers and knobs. 'They're working themselves. It's no longer under my control.'

With a great jolt that threw the Doctor back to the floor, the shuddering and bucketing stopped. Zoe was the first to the scanner.

'We're back where we started, Doctor!'

On the screen a row of what looked like sidrats stood in line.

'No,' said the Doctor. 'Those are TARDÌSes. The Time Lords have brought me home.' He went wearily to the controls and pulled the door lever. 'This is where I give myself up to their justice.'

The door opened and they all stepped into a materialisation area upon which the War Lords had modelled theirs. A tall Time Lord in long white robes was waiting for them.

'Come with me,' he said, unsmiling. He led them into a large space: not a room, for they could see no walls, yet not outside for they could see no sky. Two Time Lords, both dignified in their long robes, stood in pools of pale light. On a little dais was the War Lord.

'The witnesses have arrived,' said the Time Lord bringing in the Doctor, Jamie and Zoe. 'The trial may continue.'

'We have already discussed your crimes,' said the accusing Time Lord. 'In your selfish desire of conquest you have squandered the lives of millions of intelligent beings.'

'You call humans intelligent?' said the War Lord. 'They are primitive, always fighting among themselves.'

'What they do among themselves,' said the accusing Time Lord, 'is their own affair. We have received full details of your crime from one of our own race. Step forward, please.'

A pool of light appeared before where the Doctor was standing. He stepped into it.

'That box,' Zoe whispered to Jamie. 'That's how he told them. He put his thoughts into it.'

'Do you swear to the truth of your report?' asked a Time Lord.

'I certainly do,' said the Doctor.

A voice from someone unseen boomed down from above. 'Let me hear the defence.'

The War Lord bristled with indignation. 'First, I do not agree the authority of this court. I am War

Lord of a sovereign planet. As for this so-called witness, he collaborated with me. He captured the leaders of the human resistance for us. If I am guilty, then so is he!'

While the trial continued, two Time Lord technicians were checking over the Doctor's TARDIS. They were intrigued by its shape and puzzled by the words *Police* and *telephone* on its little windows. Their inspection was interrupted by the familiar materialisation sound. It was a common enough sound to them, but they were not expecting an arriving TARDIS. The box-like object took shape in line with the others. Strangely, its door remained closed. Curious, the two technicians went forward to investigate. Possibly the door had jammed and a Time Lord inside was trapped.

As they approached the door flew open. Five silver-uniformed security guards from the planet of the War Lords came out, firing their stun-guns and killing the two Time Lords instantly. They raced for the area where the War Lord was on trial.

The voice from above was pronouncing judgment. 'We find you guilty. That one of your party, your War Chief, was once a Time Lord gives you no excuse. Had he lived he would have been punished. Your attempt to incriminate the Time Lord who wishes to be called the Doctor is equally useless. Your crimes were monstrous and your punishment will be severe——'

The five security guards came running into the court, aiming their weapons at the Time Lords and the three witnesses. Smiling, the War Lord stepped down from his dais.

'Thank you, gentlemen. This farce is now over. We shall return to our planet.' The War Lord looked up towards the unseen voice. 'And we shall bring vengeance upon the planet of the Time Lords——'

A finger of brilliant white light stabbed down, engulfing and paralysing the War Lord where he stood.

The five guards all looked up instinctively; as they did fingers of light also fell onto them. All were frozen instantly.

'This isn't fair,' the War Lord shouted. 'After sentence there should be a right of appeal. I too could produce witnesses ... And you have no authority over me ... You have only heard half my story ...'

The great voice spoke. 'You and your murderous accomplices will be dematerialised. It will be as though you never existed.'

The six stabbing fingers of light increased in intensity. The War Lord and his security guards slowly began to fade.

'No,' screamed the War Lord. 'You don't understand. We wished to bring everlasting peace ... A New Order for the whole universe ... Peaceful coexistence, a place for you, a place for us ...'

Only the beams of light now remained. Yet the War Lord's voice, though fading, could still be heard.

'We shall win ... We shall be masters of the universe ... We have the superior intelligence ... It is our destiny to rule ...'

The lights snapped out. Not a trace remained of the War Lord and the five guards who had come to rescue him.

'Bravo,' exclaimed the Doctor. 'Good riddance.' He looked up. 'I'm glad that my evidence was so useful to the court.' He turned to Zoe and Jamie. 'Well, come along. We'd better continue with our travels.'

'No,' boomed the voice. 'You will now stand your trial. Let us hear the accusations.'

The accusing Time Lord spoke. 'The charges are two. Appropriation of a TARDIS without permission, and interference into other people's affairs. The latter is the most grave since non-interference is our most important law.'

'Well,' asked the voice. 'Do you admit these actions?'

'It isn't a very good TARDIS,' said the Doctor. 'It doesn't change shape and it won't go where I want it to go——'

'That is the lesser charge,' said the other Time Lord

present. 'What of non-interference?'

'I wanted to help people, to combat evil. Look how I've risked my life fighting the Daleks. They want to exterminate everyone. Then there are the Cybermen, a nasty lot. Do you know about the Krotons, and the Yeti? Not forgetting the Quarks and the Ice Warriors. It's true I've interfered, but always on the side of good against evil.'

'Then you admit the charge?' thundered the accusing Time Lord.

'Of course I do. But your way of observing and doing nothing, it makes life so ... so ...'

'Yes?' boomed the voice.

The Doctor looked upwards. 'It's so downright dull!'

'We have heard your defence,' said the voice. 'You will be held in custody while we consider our judgment.'

A Time Lord came forward to lead the Doctor away.

'What about my two friends?' he asked the court.

'Whatever the outcome for you,' said the voice, 'they will be well treated. You know that we are always just.'

'Yes,' said the Doctor, hanging his head. 'I know only too well.'

The cell was small and windowless. Its doorway had no door; instead a force field made escape seemingly impossible. The Doctor was pacing up and down when a Time Lord came down the passageway with Jamie and Zoe.

'I've brought your friends to say goodbye.'

Jamie offered his hand to the Doctor, only to find that it banged against the force field across the doorway.

'Can't we go inside to say goodbye?' asked Zoe. 'We shall probably never see him again.'

The Time Lord looked at the tears welling up in Zoe's eyes. 'All right,' he said. 'But I shall have to confine you in there with him.'

He crossed to the opposite wall. His hands flickered over a small panel of intricate symbols. 'Go in,' he said.

Jamie and Zoe entered the cell. Immediately they were inside, the Time Lord's fingers flickered again over the symbols. 'I shall leave you to talk in private,' he said, and slowly went back down the passageway.

'I think your Time Lords are awful,' said Jamie. 'They're so strait-laced.'

'Don't be too harsh on them,' said the Doctor. 'They're good people really.' He sighed. 'It's because they're so good that I left them!'

'I think it's time you left them again,' said Zoe.

'Easier said than done, my dear.'

'I don't know ...' She was wriggling her toe against the bottom of the force field. 'Jamie's hand banged into it higher up, but my toe can go right through at the bottom.'

'That's the molecular distortion effect at ground level,' the Doctor explained. 'But it's very slight.'

'If I lay flat on my back, could you two push me through? I'm very thin.'

'Maybe we could,' said Jamie. 'That'd leave the Doctor and me stuck in here.'

'Except,' said Zoe, 'I memorised what that Time Lord did to that little panel of symbols over there. Want to try?'

'You're a genius,' said the Doctor. 'Quick—get down.'

Zoe lay flat, hands stretched above her head like a diver. She held her body rigid while Jamie and the Doctor pushed.

'There,' she said, springing to her feet on the other side. 'Let's see if I can remember exactly what that Time Lord did ...' Her fingers played across the little panel.

In his eagerness for escape Jamie was leaning against the force field when its power was cut. He fell forward, and was saved by the Doctor.

'All we have to do now,' said the Doctor, 'is try to

find where they keep all those TARDISes.'

They started to run.

The TARDIS still looked like an old-fashioned London police box.

'I can't believe we've made it,' said Jamie, pausing to catch his breath.

'Since it isn't yours anyway,' Zoe said to the Doctor, 'why not take one of the better ones? One that will change to look like different things; one that you can really direct.'

The Doctor shook his head. 'All my things are in the old TARDIS. It's become home. Come on, let's get into it.'

They had but a few steps to go when the light stabbed down on them. They could not move. Time Lords approached from each end of the materialisation area.

'There is no escape, Doctor,' said one. 'It is time to say goodbye to your friends.'

'Doctor,' said Jamie, 'not after all we've been through.'

'Please, Doctor,' said Zoe, tears running down her cheeks. 'Plead with them to let us stay with you.'

The light trapping them had gone out, but they were surrounded by robed Time Lords.

'It's no good,' said the Doctor, taking Jamie's hand. 'This has to be goodbye. Don't go blundering into too much trouble.' He turned to Zoe and hugged her. 'Goodbye, my dear.'

'Will we never see you again?' she asked in a tiny voice.

'Who knows,' said the Doctor. 'Time is relative. Please, leave me now, and no fuss.'

The Doctor turned away from Jamie and Zoe. Three Time Lords closed in to escort him back to the court.

'They will both forget me?' he asked.

'Not entirely,' said a Time Lord. 'They will be returned to a moment in time just before they went away with you. They will remember only their first adventure with you, but nothing else.'

'Has my fate been decided yet?'

'It has,' said the Time Lord. 'You will be told by the court.'

A large screen hung from nowhere.

'Your friend the girl,' said the great voice. 'We thought you would wish to see her safe return. Watch.'

The Doctor looked up at the screen. A great wheel-shaped space ship appeared against a backdrop of the twinkling galaxy.

'She is already on the way in a TARDIS,' said the voice. 'She is about to arrive.'

The image changed to a curved corridor inside the wheel in space. Zoe came walking along, her expression a little vague and puzzled. A man came towards her.

'Zoe! Are you all right?'

She looked at the man blankly. 'Yes.'

'Have the Doctor and Jamie gone?'

'Yes ... I've just seen them off.'

'Well,' said the man, 'we'd better get back to work. Are you sure you're all right?'

She hesitated. 'For a moment I thought I'd forgotten something important. But it's nothing.'

'Come along, then,' said the man. He started off down the corridor.

'All right. I'm coming.' She paused and frowned. Then she shook her head, as though discarding some memory, and followed the man. The screen went blank.

'Thank you,' said the Doctor. 'It was considerate of you to let me see that she's all right.'

The voice spoke again. 'The young man, Jamie, has just arrived back on his planet. Again you may watch.'

The screen showed Scottish moorland. The de-materialisation sound of a TARDIS could be heard. Jamie picked himself up from the heather where the Time Lords had laid him. He rubbed his forehead as he regained his senses. A shot rang out. Some distance

141

away a solitary English redcoat had fired at Jamie. Quickly looking round, Jamie picked up a large piece of wood.

'Try to murder a Macrimon, would you! You'll pay for that, Englishman!'

The redcoat, unable to re-load his single-shot rifle before Jamie bore down on him, took to his heels. Jamie went after him gleefully waving his make-do claymore. The picture faded.

'As for the soldiers,' said the voice, 'they are being returned to their home times as fast as possible.'

'I'm grateful,' said the Doctor.

'And now,' said the voice, 'the question of what to do with you. What do you expect us to do with you?'

The Doctor thought. 'Dematerialisation?'

'We are not savages.'

'Perhaps you will sentence me to work in the archives for the next thousand years, something boring like that.'

'No,' said the voice. 'We accept there is evil that must be fought, and that you still have a part to play in that battle.'

The Doctor couldn't believe his ears. 'You're going to set me free?'

'Not entirely. We have noted your interest in the planet Earth. You seem to have a special knowledge of that world and its problems.'

'I suppose I have,' said the Doctor. 'Earth seems particularly vulnerable to attack by other worlds.'

'For that reason you will be sent back to that planet, in exile.'

'Exile?'

'You will remain there for such time as we deem proper. During that time the secret of the TARDIS will be taken from you.'

'Surely,' the Doctor pleaded, 'you can't condemn me to exile on one primitive planet! Besides I'm known on Earth already. It will be very difficult for me.'

'Your appearance has changed before: it will change again.'

'You can't change what I look like without consulting me!'

'Here is your first choice,' said the voice. On the screen appeared a man's face—sunken cheeks, hair white, dull eyes.

'Good gracious,' exclaimed the Doctor. 'Too old!'

The first picture was replaced with another.

'No, never! Too thin.'

Another picture appeared.

'Too young. No one would respect me ...'

'You are wasting time,' said the great voice.

'It's not my fault, is it? Is this the best you can do? I've never seen such a collection.'

'The decision will be taken for you.'

'This is preposterous! I have a right to decide what I look like. People on Earth attach great importance to appearance ...'

As he spoke the Doctor vanished from where he had been standing. It was now his face that filled the screen. He looked down angrily.

'Is this some sort of joke? Put me back where I was!'

The great voice said, 'The time has come for you to change your appearance and to begin your exile. There will be no further discussion.'

'I refuse to be treated like this,' said the Doctor. 'What are you doing now?'

The Doctor's face on the screen had begun to revolve, first slowly then fast.

'Stop!' his voice cried out. 'You're making me giddy ... I won't have it! You can't do this to me!'

The image of the Doctor's face spun faster and faster until it became a blur. Finally the screen went blank and the Doctor's voice was heard no more.

The accusing Time Lord looked upwards. 'I think you did right. He would never have fitted in back here.'

'I agree,' said the great voice. 'It's a pity. He would have brightened the place up no end.'